THE WITCHER UNIVERSE: ORDER OF BOOKS, CHARACTERS, KINGDOMS, BESTIARY

& More from the book series by Andrzej Sapkowski

Ted West

Disclaimer: All names, brands, avatars, and photos were replaced with fictitious ones. To avoid copyright infringement. This did not affect the comicality of the situations described in the book.

All characters appearing in this book are fictitious. Any resemblance to real persons, living or dead, is purely coincidental.

This book is for educational purposes only. The views expressed are those of the author alone. The reader is responsible for his or her own actions. Adherence to all applicable laws and regulations, including international, federal, state, and local governing professional licensing, business practices, advertising, and all other aspects of doing business in the United States, Canada, or any other jurisdiction, is the sole responsibility of the purchaser or reader. Neither the author nor the publisher assumes any responsibility or liability whatsoever on behalf of the purchaser or reader of these materials.

CONTENTS

Foreword

Did you like The Witcher from Netflix or the game universe from CD Project and now want to immerse yourself in Andrzej Sapkowski's books The Witcher? Or maybe you are already a fan of the book series and want to recollect or structure information from the Saga? Either way, you've come to the right place.

This guide contains interesting knowledge about breathtaking places and deadly monsters that live there, the main heroes and their exploits.

Monsters are presented in the bestiary section, where there is information about the most important and interesting monsters that are encountered while reading books or playing through the game.

The guide briefly depicts the politics, formation, and population of the kingdoms to give fans a better understanding of the events. A map is also present.

Of course, a diagram of the order to read the books is presented, which will allow you to read novels correctly without spoilers.

Here is a summary of the guide:

- the order of reading the Witcher books;
- description of important events that influenced the history of the Witcher's world;
- bestiary;
- location, economy, and politics of kingdoms;
- races, their history of origin and settlement on the continent;
- characteristics of the characters of the Saga;
- and others.

All this will help you better understand the story. You will easily navigate the Witcher universe and better understand the actions of the heroes! Geographical objects, monsters, and character names will not cause confusion; you will like this vast universe.

The encyclopedia will serve as an excellent addition to the books and the Witcher series of games and is a must in the collection of every true fan of this epic dark fantasy from Andrzej Sapkowski!

Enjoy!

Thank You for Purchasing & Reading!

I hope you find the information useful and easy to use.

1. THE WITCHER SAGA

With the Witcher Netflix series out now (and quite good!) and The Witcher 3 seeing more concurrent players than ever, there's a lot of renewed interest in the root of all this: The Witcher books. If you want to fill a Geralt-shaped hole in your life following the show and games, the books are definitely worth a read.

It's not quite as easy as one, two, three, though. Let's start from the beginning, all right?

* * *

"The Witcher Saga" (Polish: "Saga o wiedźminie") is a fantasy series of novels by Polish writer Andrzej Sapkowski.

The first short story of the series was published in 1986 and the last one in 2013. The book takes place in a fictional world reminiscent of Europe in the late Middle Ages, where all kinds of magical creatures and monsters exist, along with people. Geralt of Rivia is one of the last Witcher, monster hunters.

The first books of the series are collections of stories about the adventures of Geralt, where folklore and classic literary tales are often satirically played out. The plot of the subsequent books is a larger story, built around Geralt and his foster-daughter Ciri, who possesses magical powers.

The books have been adapted into two TV series - Polish (2002) and American (2019), as well as a fan movie, "Half a century of poetry later"; computer games: ("The Witcher," "The Witcher 2: Assassins of Kings" and "The Witcher 3: Wild Hunt"); a rock opera written and staged; comic books about the adventures of Geralt and other characters of the saga were published in the writer's homeland.

2. PLOT

The main character of the series is Geralt of Rivia, a Witcher, who makes a living by hunting monsters that pose a threat to people's lives. As a child, like other Witchers, he survived mutations, thanks to which he gained great fighting skills: increased strength, speed of reaction, accelerated metabolism, but at the same time, lost the ability to have children.

Geralt's main job is to destroy dangerous monsters for money. However, he is not always ready to mindlessly fulfill the orders of his employers. For example, he refuses to destroy creatures with high intelligence, or dragons that are threatened with extinction.

In accordance with his own code of behavior, he tries not to participate in the political intrigues of kings and wizards but eventually becomes involved in a complex tie of confrontation between the Northern kingdoms and the powerful southern Empire of Nilfgaard. Geralt tries to protect his adopted daughter and the young Princess of the ruined Kingdom of Cintra, Ciri (child of Surprise), destined for him before her birth. Ciri becomes the focus of the interests of influential forces (Emperor of Nilfgaard, sorcerer Vilgefortz, The Lodge of Sorceresses) since her descendant is predicted to decide the fate of the world. Having received symbolic gifts-skills from her adoptive parents (Geralt and his beloved, the sorceress Yennefer): Witcher's - sword playing and sorcerer's - magic abilities; undergoing further hardships, Ciri becomes the main character of the saga, along with Geralt.

3. BOOKS

Which Book Should I Read First?

"The Last Wish" is the first book you should read when starting this series. Although it was not the first Witcher book published, it contains stories that take place before the original novel. This book establishes the backdrop of the Continent. The story introduces readers to Geralt before explaining what Witchers are and do. In this book, Geralt fights in bars, tames beasts, and seduces women.

The Witcher stories give a backstory to the things seen in the video games that they're based on. Andrzej Sapkowski, the author, talks about the silver sword of Geralt, which he uses to destroy the "Monsters of Magic." You will learn about how corrupt the governments are all over the world, as well as be introduced to an ensemble cast of characters, including the following:

- ➢ Jaskier (Dandelion), Geralt's friend who listens to the tales we hear. Jaskier is a poet.
- ➢ Yennefer, a woman who specializes in sorcery, and who is in a relationship with Geralt, albeit a troubled one.
- ➢ Triss, another one of Geralt's friends, who also develops a relationship with Geralt, causing conflict with Yennefer.

Sword of Destiny is the next collection of short stories to be read in sequence. In the story, we are introduced to Ciri. Each story in Sword of Destiny transpires right before the primary books.

4. WHY SHOULD I READ THEM?

- You'll finally understand all the references Geralt and other characters are constantly making to past events.
- They'll provide you with a lot of in-depth background information on the world and characters.
- You'll actually understand who the hell everyone is.
- Random names of places like Kovir, Nilfgaard, Cintra, Kaedwen, etc. will actually mean something to you.
- You'll care about the characters and the story significantly more.
- **They're just damn good books.**

5. READING ORDER

- The Last Wish.
- Sword of Destiny.
- Season of Storms (though this is optional, as explained below).
- Blood of Elves.
- Time of Contempt.
- Baptism of Fire.
- The Tower of the Swallow.
- The Lady of the Lake.

After the Witcher's short stories are read, most people would assume that the remainder of these books could be read in the sequence they were released in. However, Season of Storms, which was recently released, transpires during the events of "The Last Wish."

Season of Storms is not mandatory reading, but you can read it if you really want to dive deep into this series. With that said, the events that transpire in this book are not crucial to the central arc. Rather, it plants storyline seeds that will be of significance in later chapters.

There were also stories written: "The Road with No Return" (Polish: Droga, z ktorej sie nie wraca) (1988) and "Something Ends, Something Begins" (Polish: Coś się kończy, coś się zaczyna) (1992), not directly related to the Witcher series, but whose action takes place in the same universe.

The story, "The Road with No Return" describes the alleged parents of the Witcher, in particular, his mother, Visenna, and a possible father. "Something Ends, Something Begins" presents an alternative, non-canonical ending to the saga— Sapkowski calls it a "self-written fan fiction."

During the Warsaw Comic-Con festival, which was held from April 20-24, 2018, Andrzej Sapkowski announced that he was working on a new book of "The Witcher" series.

5.1 WHERE CAN I GET THEM?

1. The Last Wish. 1993

The Last Wish – this collection of short stories introduces Geralt as a Witcher. His targets tend to be vile fiends and multifarious monsters who attack innocents and ravage lands. Not all evil is easy to spot, though.

2. Sword Of Destiny. 1993

Sword of Destiny – this collection of short stories has Geralt roaming the nation in search of assignments. Over time, he realizes that – although a significant portion of his quarries is vicious, violent, and grotesque, others tend to be evil, naïve, or sinful.

3. Season Of Storms. 2013

Season of Storms – after a contract goes wrong, Geralt loses the signature weapons he depends on. He will require them as a storm is brewing, and sorcerers have bad intentions for the coming days...

4. Blood Of Elves. 1994

Blood of Elves – elves, gnomes, dwarfs, and humans have lived together in peace for more than a century. But change is in the works – peace is off the table, and races begin fighting with each other. Meanwhile, Geralt anticipates a supposedly prophesized child's birth. Apparently, the power this child will have is capable of making the world either evil or good. With threats of war looming over the country, people begin hunting the child in order to capitalize on its powers. Geralt is responsible for protecting everyone involved.

5. Time Of Contempt. 1995

Time of Contempt – nonhumans and elves continue to suffer after decades of being repressed. Some of them join commando units that are hidden deep inside the forest - these soldiers strike at will before disappearing within the trees. Against this contempt and fear backdrop, Geralt and Yennefer, his lover, seek to protect Ciri, an orphaned heir who is being chased by just about everyone. A prophecy is resting on her, as the girl has the potential to save or end the world, whether she's dead or alive.

6. Baptism Of Fire. 1996

Baptism of Fire – a coup has shattered the Wizards' Guild. During the uproar, Geralt sustained serious injuries. Now that the world has fallen into dark times, he remains helpless and needs time to recover. As war wreaks havoc throughout the land, magic's future becomes threatened, and the surviving sorcerers endeavor to keep it protected.

7. The Tower Of The Swallow. 1997

War has ravaged the world, and Ciri has disappeared. Hunted by both foes and friends alike, she lives her life with freedom under the disguise of a bandit – a freedom she has never tasted before. However, Ciri is oblivious to the fact that her days of freedom are numbered. Geralt assembles a team of allies charged with saving her. Each side involved in the war has sent out burial mercenaries to find her. The crimes he has committed have caught the attention of a lot of people. The only place she can go…is the Tower of Swallows.

8. Lady Of The Lake. 1999

Barely escaping death, Ciri is thrown into the world of elves, a place completely unfamiliar to her. Ciri is trapped there and doesn't have any way to get out. Time doesn't exist in this place, and she doesn't have any access to portals or borders that can get

her home.

That doesn't mean she will be defeated, though. She is the child of a prophecy, after all.

5.2 BOOK RATING

Following readers' ratings on Goodreads.com, The Witcher series is surprisingly consistent in terms of quality.

"Season of Storms," originally published 14 years after Sapkowski ended his saga, has reached the bottom, suggesting that some of the author's magic has dissipated over the years. The five books translated by David French are ahead of Danusia Stok's two books, suggesting that readers may prefer French's style.

But given that even the lowest rating gets a very respectable 3.95 out of 5, fantasy fans are unlikely to be disappointed with any of Sapkowski's novels.

- "Sword of Destiny" — 4.35.
- "Baptism of Fire" — 4.34.
- "The Tower of the Swallow" — 4.32.
- "Time of Contempt" — 4.26.
- "The Lady of the Lake" — 4.24.
- "The Last Wish" — 4.19.
- "Blood of Elves" — 4.16.
- "Season of Storms" — 3.95.

6. UNDERSTANDING THE WITCHER UNIVERSE

Background

These stories take place on a Continent that has no name, which was settled thousands of years ago by elves who came from overseas. Once they arrived, these elves came across dwarves and gnomes.

A war took place between the dwarves and elves. In the end, the dwarves fled for the mountains, while the elves started residing in the forests and the plains. Approximately 500 years prior to the events that took place in the stories, humans colonists invaded the lands, which resulted in many wars. In the end, the humans won and became the dominant race.

The non-human races were now seen as second-class citizens and lived inside small ghettos that were within the human settlements, while the others lived in the wilderness regions that haven't been claimed by the humans. Some other races present on the Continent are dryads and halflings. Plus, vampires and werewolves showed up after a magical event took place, which was called the Conjunction of the Spheres.

A couple of centuries before the events in the stories occurred, the majority of the southern regions of the Continent were conquered by the Nilfgaard Empire, while the northern regions belonged to the Northern Kingdoms. The Aftermath of the first great war between the Northern Kingdoms and the Nilfgaard Empire is when The Witcher saga begins. Soon enough, the second war occurs in the middle of The Witcher series.

7. CULTURE

Below is a description of the main concepts that influenced the Witcher universe.

* * *

7.1 WHITE FROST

White Frost — the name of one of the omens of the end of the world and one of its causes, appearing in the prophecy of the elven knowledgeable Ithlinne.

Description

According to Ithlinne, after the beginning of the destruction of the world and its inhabitants, due to a number of circumstances, those who survive will be destroyed by the frost.

Origin

There are various theories of the origin and nature of White Frost, in particular, linking the Cataclysm with ordinary and explicable climate changes or with some magical phenomenon. Avallac'h interpreted White Frost as a poetic metaphor for the approach of the ice age, which will occur as a result of changes in the orbit and axis of the planet, which, in turn, will lead to a significant shift in the permafrost boundary, shifts of the Northern glaciers to the South and the subsequent glaciation of the continent.

In The game The Witcher 3: Wild Hunt, the concept changes somewhat, and White Frost becomes a kind of magical (although, in fact, magic is part of nature in a broad sense) phenomenon, and this phenomenon has an epicenter from which it spreads throughout the universe. And the phenomenon inevitably and necessarily destroys all life on each planet at one stage or another of the existence of intelligent life, and it fills the void between the worlds.

The Rescue

Neither magic nor even the talents of the elven wizards Aen Saevherne can prevent a Cataclysm, although the elves can temporarily slow the progress of the glaciation. Avallac'h, following a certain hypothesis accepted by his people, assumed that people would be able to survive the disaster due to high adaptability, while the elves could only be saved if they went for Swallow, i.e., for Elder Blood – the incredible abilities of its carrier would allow them to open Ard Gaeth and go to another world, unaffected by White Frost.

Even though the only supposed escape from this cataclysm is flight, in The game The Witcher 3: Wild Hunt, in some or perhaps even all scenarios, Ciri manages to destroy the epicenter of White Frost, thereby stopping the death of worlds and races.

7.2 ELDER SPEECH

Elder Speech is a fictional language with a runic script, which is spoken in the works of the Witcher cycle, the language of the ancient people of the elves.

The language is based, in particular, on existing Welsh, German, French, English, Irish, and Latin. It is quite difficult to learn a language, although it is possible. It is also used as the main magic language.

Types of pronunciation:

- Classic.
- "Singing" (sirens, dryads, and nereids).

7.3 ETERNAL FIRE

Eternal Fire is the main Novigrad cult, widespread in many Northern kingdoms.

Essence

The personification of Eternal Fire is any manifestation of fire. According to the belief, Eternal Fire is the essence of all living things. The cult is based on the dominant male principle. This explains the fact that the main priestly positions in the hierarchy of the cult are held by men.

Followers of the cult are obliged to observe holidays and rituals, fervently believe in religious dogmas, observe the rules, and pray.

Hierarchy

The hierarchical structure of the cult is as follows:

The cult is headed by a hierarch. By tradition, the main temple of Eternal Fire and the location of the hierarch is the city of Novigrad, a city-state in Redania. This state of affairs is because Redania is the mainstay of the cult (about 80% of the population supports the belief in Eternal Fire).

On the territory of other states, the head of the cult is vicars — the leader of the cult in this state. The vicars are subordinate to the hierarch.

Lower in the hierarchy are the priests of the cult. As a rule, in cities and localities, there are one or more priests whose duties include taking care of the spiritual well-being of the flock, performing services and rituals, and expanding the ranks of believers.

Next are the adepts (monks) of the cult. They help the priests, take care of the temples, and help the faithful.

Armed Forces

The armed unit of Eternal Fire is the Order of the White Rose. The order is a knightly military formation. The original task of the order was to protect the priests of the cult, temple buildings, and protect the faithful. However, the Order was rapidly losing its position, growing discontent, mainly based on the lack of "purity" and idealism in the ranks of the knights because it was possible to purchase the status of a knight, which opened the way for a "dubious" class of people. And most of the knights began to relate to the mission of the cult without due zeal, and because of this, both the reputation of the Order and, accordingly, the reputation of the cult were greatly shaken.

The order is headed by the Grand Master, who reports directly to the hierarch.

Subsequently, the Order of the White Rose was replaced by the Order of the Flaming Rose, led by Jacques de Aldersberg. After the elimination of the Order of the Flaming Rose, Witch Hunters became the cult's new fighting force.

7.4 LAW OF SURPRISE

The Law of Surprise is a custom known throughout the Northern Kingdoms. Any person or being has the right to demand the Law of Surprise for any service from a person (being) unfamiliar to him.

Despite the apparent conditionality, after taking an oath and subject to a number of conditions, this right guarantees its owner to get what he wants, even after a long period of time.

Variants of requirements:

1. (A person / being) is given what is the first to meet (a person / being), who took an oath on the threshold of his house.
2. (The person / being) is given what (the person / being) does not know and does not expect to see at home.
3. (The person / being) is given what (the person / being) already has, but what he does not know about when he returns home.

7.5 TRIAL OF THE GRASSES

Trial of the Grasses — the second stage of Witchers training. The Herb trial is one of the most common myths about Witchers. The test involves the introduction of specific elixirs into the body under constant magical control, which radically changes the human metabolism, hormonal and nervous systems. Trial of the Grasses —is an extremely dangerous process, and out of ten subjected to it, on average, four or three survive. After the Trial of the Grasses, the Witchers will have to go through the third stage of training — eye mutation.

After the attack on Caer Morhen by an army of fanatics and the destruction of most of the Witchers, wizards, and apprentices present there, the training of Witchers is no longer conducted, due to the loss of the knowledge necessary to carry out the most serious mutations and wizards able to control the entire process.

And with the death of the old Witcher Vesemir, the only person who knows the entire procedure of The test, the hope of reviving the profession of Witchers disappeared completely. However, shortly before his death, he took part in the Transmutations program that young students used to take to give the Avallac'h cursed by Eredin a normal appearance.

8. EVENTS

Before starting to list all the memorable events that occurred in this fictional world, it should be noted that many dates are approximate values because, in the novel itself, the author does not give direct dates for some events that occurred before the beginning of the Saga of the Adventures of White Wolf.

Plus, with the release of the Witcher games, there were some inconsistencies in the dates of events that ended the main story of the book Saga and began the plot of the game series. Also, events are described superficially to avoid spoilers.

* * *

8.1 CONJUNCTION OF THE SPHERES

The Conjunction of the Spheres is a famous magical cataclysm that occurred about 1,500 years ago. Conjugation affected a whole chain of worlds, partly mixed their boundaries, and made them easily surmountable for a short time. Thanks to this, people appeared in the world of the Witcher, and many creatures that did not belong to this world were trapped in it. Therefore, for example, ghouls, vampires do not have their own ecological niche. They are relics of the Conjunction of the Spheres period. Their spread led to the emergence of professional hunters for them - mutant Witchers.

Scientific Description

Supposedly, at least three worlds participated in the Conjunction of the Spheres cataclysm. The first world, obviously, is the homeland of people whose world died as a result of some catastrophe, as a result of which people had to look for a new home. The second world is the world of the Witcher, where people, elves, dwarves, gnomes, evil spirits, and, possibly, someone else have got.

The fact that at least one other world participated in the Conjunction of the Spheres is proved by the fact that there are many species that do not have their place in the food chain. But from the original world of people, such creatures could not get because they are mostly of a magical nature, and people before Conjunction of the Spheres did not know magic.

8.2 FALKA'S REBELLION

Falka's Rebellion (1157-1158 (59)) - tragic and bloody events that took place on the territory of the Northern Kingdoms.

Course Of Events

Falka, the first-born daughter of the King of Redania, set out to seize the throne at all costs, which, she believed by right belonged to her. Soon, the struggle for the throne escalated into a peasant war that engulfed colossal territories. The brutality of Falka and her supporters became legendary, although most likely, she simply lost control of the situation and was no longer able to curb the out of control anger of the rabble.

In the process of the uprising, Falka killed her father, his wife, and two half brothers with her own hands. Falka's rebels have captured and concluded at Houtborg Castle the pregnant Redanian princess Riannon, consort of Goidemar.

Ultimately, the uprising was depressed by the Temerian army led by Goidemar, and Falka was burned at the stake.

8.3 NORTHERN WAR I

Northern War I — the first attempt of the Nilfgaard Empire to subdue the Northern Kingdoms.

Nilfgaard conquered Cintra, Attre, Lower Sodden, Riverdell, and Angren — all lands South of Yaruga. It is not known for sure whether there was any peace that ended this phase of fighting between Nilfgaard and the nordlings.

8.4 THE BATTLE OF CINTRA

The Battle of Cintra or Slaughter of Cintra — a four-day battle for the city of Cintra, which took place in the late summer of 1263, during the invasion of the Nilfgaard Empire in the Kingdom of the same name. It ended with the fall of the city and the death of most of the defenders.

8.5 NORTHERN WAR II

Northern War II — the second attempt of the Nilfgaard Empire to subdue the Northern Kingdoms. The official start of the second Northern Kingdoms war with Nilfgaard is considered to be the attack of the Nilfgaard army on Lyria and Aedirn in 1267.

Northern War II ended with the so-called Peace of Cintra, a Peace Treaty signed by Nilfgaard and the Northern Kingdoms on April 2, 1268.

8.6 RIVIAN POGROM

The Rivian Pogrom is an infamous event that took place in the city of Rivia in 1268. An act of racism and xenophobia instigated by Nadia Esposito. It claimed 184 lives (half of them were women and children).

8.7 WITCH HUNTS

The witch hunts-bloody persecution of sorceresses, alchemists, village wizards, sorcerers, and magical creatures, which lasted from 1272 to 1276. It caused the death of many people, most of whom were not related to magic. Many members of the Elder Races also died during the hunt. Victims were impaled or burned at the stake. The main organizers of the terror were the Hierarch of Eternal Fire Cyrus Engelkind Hemmelfart, the priest Willemer and the king of Redania Radovid.

To fight the mages, witch hunters units were created, the backbone of the organization was the former Order of the Flaming Rose, whose units soon flooded Novigrad and Redania. Their task was to track down, capture, and execute any person who was suspected of magical acts. That's how, in just a few months, Novigrad went from being the cultural center of the North to a city of anger and hatred, with rivers of innocent people's blood washing its streets and the smoke of bonfires permeating the air.

8.8 NORTHERN WAR III

Northern War III is the third attempt by the Nilfgaard empire to conquer the Northern Kingdoms. The war that takes place during the game The Witcher 3: Wild Hunt.

The war could end in complete triumph for the Southern Invader if King Radovid V is killed and the player sided with Roche. If King Radovid is alive, or the player has supported Dijkstra, then Redania will give a good rebuff to Nilfgaard.

9. RACES

No real fantasy world is complete without elves, dwarfs, gnomes, and other non-human races. It is a genre definition element. It would seem that it is difficult to avoid often commonplace stereotypes, such as noble elves, stubborn dwarfs, or ordinary people.

Despite this, Andrzej Sapkowski showed that it is possible. Creating his own version of the fantasy world, he brought a huge amount of novelty to the beaten-up genre. The author achieved this by looking at the problems of modern society from an unusual perspective and then transferring his views to the fantasy universe.

* * *

9.1 HUMAN

Human is the youngest race on the continent. They landed around 764 at the mouths of the Yaruga and Pontar rivers, resulting in the formation of the first three states: Temeria, Redania, and Cintra. Common Speech also appeared on the continent with their arrival.

History

However, as it turned out, the world was already densely populated, and the bulk of the population were nonhumans: Elves, Gnomes, Dwarves, Halflings, who also call themselves Elder Folk. Their main difference from human aliens was in their life span by human standards, comparable to eternity.

After the landing began the colonization of land by people. And here we find another difference with nonhumans — the ability to reproduce quickly.

In the course of history, mixed races appear: half-elves, quarter-elves, and the like, but their relatives call them traitors.

Humans were distinguished by their belligerence, selfishness, and hypocrisy, and were prone to racism. Therefore, the colonization of the lands was accompanied by the extermination or pushing back of the Elder Folk (the war of 1050 ended with the Battle of Shaerrawedd). This is how the "reservations" of nonhumans appeared, and the human began to settle in the places of elven cities (Novigrad, Oxenfurt, Vizima, Tretogor, Maribor, Cidaris, Cintra, and many others).

9.2 ELDER RACES

Elder Races is a generic term used by elves to describe the intelligent races that inhabited the continent before the arrival of humans.

They include:

- Gnomes.
- Halflings.
- Dwarves.
- Vrans.
- Elves.
- Dryads.

Humans call these peoples simply nonhumans. Of all these races, the gnomes and halflings are the oldest peoples on the continent (but most likely, they lived either at the same time or before the Vrans), appearing thousands of years before the Conjunction of the Spheres and the arrival of the elves and humans on the continent.

9.3 ELVES

The Elves are a highly developed humanoid race with pointed ears and a rich culture. Some of the representatives of Elder Folk.

History

Once all the Elves were part of a single people, Aen Undod, which existed long before the Conjunction of the Spheres. After an unknown disaster destroyed their homeworld, Aen Undod began searching for new worlds. Their descendants were divided into two different groups — Aen Elle, who conquered one of the worlds and occupied it, and Aen Seidhe, who sailed on their White Ships to the Continent at the very beginning of our era, two centuries after the Conjunction of the Spheres, nine hundred years before humans and millennia later gnomes and halflings. It is from the moment of arrival on the Continent of Aen Seidhe that the years of our era begin.

General information:

- **Origin**: the Elves believe that they were created, unlike humans, who evolved. Therefore, some of the elves consider humans to be nothing more than hairless apes.
- **Appearance**: Generally, the elves are very handsome. They have pointed ears, sharp facial features, and no fangs. The latter clearly indicates a non-animal origin.
- **Life Span**: These centenarians, by human standards, live almost forever, and their incomparable beauty does not fade over time. For example, Aen Seidhe lived for about three

hundred years, and Aen Elle lived up to six hundred years.

- **Abilities / Traits**: Many Elves are extremely powerful mages, assisted by their innate magical abilities, and reflexes and resilience make elven archers the best on the Continent.

- **Culture**: over the centuries, the Elves have created a beautiful and sophisticated culture. Elves are perfect in almost everything — they firmly believe in their superiority. Their culture symbolizes calmness, seriousness, and control of their emotions.

9.4 DWARVES

Dwarves - short, sturdy, stocky Elder Folk, outwardly similar to people. Mostly warriors, artisans, and merchants. Dwarves are long-livers, like elves; however, among them, only "youth" are fertile. Women-dwarves are described very little; we can say there is no description of them at all in books or games, but it is known that they are not very attractive by human standards (unlike elves, whose beauty is very revered by people).

History

The book does not describe when or how the dwarves appeared on the mainland. It is known that they settled here before hu mans and Elves, but later gnomes. Obviously, the dwarves managed to make friends with gnomes, and these races learned a lot from each other, but when the elves sailed to the continent on their White ships, these two peoples were forced into the bowels of the mountains.

Culture

Unlike many humans, elves and Witchers, dwarves use heavy weapons most often: maces, clubs, axes. However, they use this weapon quite deftly, and can easily throw at a great distance if necessary. The main habitat of the dwarves is the Mahakam massif enclave. Most of their forges and laboratories are located here.

When the colonization of the lands by the people who arrived on the continent began, the dwarves got along with people quite calmly. Many settled in the cities and went about their business: trade, forging weapons. In the regular armies of almost all kingdoms, dwarves were far from the last place, thanks to their high military training.

9.5 GNOMES

Gnomes are very small creatures with elongated pointed ears and a long nose. Perhaps, after the wrans, it is the oldest race in the world. They are a very strange and secretive race. In cities outside of Mahakam, gnomes are incredibly rare. They mostly live in the mountains of Tir Tochair.

Appearance

Dwarves and gnomes are related races; they live in very similar conditions, have similar activities, and both races are mainly engaged in metallurgy and mining from the mines. Both races have a similar clan structure of society. However, there are also differences in appearance: dwarves are larger than gnomes (dwarven height is 1.25-1.4 meters, and the gnome is 0.85-1.05 m tall) and more stocky. Dwarves wear a beard, but the gnome does not always, and if it does, it cuts it short.

Another significant difference in the appearance of the races is the nose. Gnomes always have long noses, twice as long as the noses of dwarves and humans.

9.6 HALFLINGS

The Halflings are one of the non-human races in The Witcher's world. Absolutely classic, short, curly barefoot lovers of comfort and dense food.

Appearance

Unlike wide and dumpy dwarves, they look quite proportional, only their facial features at any age retain the softness characteristic of children of other races. Described rather superficially, from the available data, it can be concluded that they were mainly engaged in agriculture, in which they were quite successful, as well as in trade.

9.7 DRYADS

Dryads-beautiful and proud female warriors who live in the forest of Brokilon. Where are the sacred caves of Craag An and Duen Canell-the abode of the high priestess dryads, who protects ancient traditions.

Appearance

Dryads are very beautiful, although they are strikingly different from the canons that people are used to. In the original source, there is no mention of their skin color, only that true Dryads are similar in appearance to elves (tall, small teeth, etc.). In the game universe, they have a greenish skin that helps them blend perfectly with the foliage of trees, and their hair color fluctuates between the color of cinnamon and emerald green. The facial features are very sharp, the faces narrow, as well as very light sinewy bodies.

Features

It is noteworthy that dryads, as well as other similar creatures, do not have males - no one has ever seen male dryads. They make love only for the sake of reproduction. They reproduce by making love with the best - in the opinion of dryads - representatives of other races, wishing to pass on the strength, stability, and the best genetic material of the selected males to the future generation. In addition, dryads take human girls, thrown or lost in the forest, into their ranks. To do this, they use water from a special Brokilon source, which has toxic properties. After taking water, girls forget their whole past life and from that moment, they are raised as dryads.

9.8 VRANS

The Vrans are an ancient race that formed the first civilization and lived in the world long before the elves and humans appeared. Outwardly, they look like huge intelligent humanoid lizards with large red eyes. They are considered extinct.

Several sorcerers have speculated that the vrans are relics of the Conjunction of the Spheres, but no evidence has been found.

A certain number of vrans once lived in the ancient city of Loc Muinne, but then mysteriously and almost simultaneously, all died. According to the records of the scientist Aep Dearhenna, there is an assumption that vrans could have contracted various diseases from elves or died from climate change. And Vernon Roche suggests that the vrans may have been killed by weapons since many hacked-up lizard skeletons were found under the city.

9.9 VODYANOY

Vodyanoy is a sentient underwater race of creatures, carefully guarding their own secrets and secrets. They live at the bottom of the seas and oceans. Outwardly, they look like fish-like humanoids and have their own language, culture and religion. They know how to handle metals.

9.10 DRAGONS

Dragons — very rare flying intelligent creatures that have the appearance of a lizard. It is assumed that they represent the forces of Chaos, which seek to destroy everything on the continent. Dragons are creatures that can absorb magical energy from nature. Using the received force, the dragons, for some unknown reason, use it to gather untold riches in their lair. After their passion is satisfied, the dragon falls into lethargy for a long time before the first appearance of an external stimulus.

There is nothing more disgusting for dragons than humans. A man awakens instinctive, irrational disgust in dragons. The emerging conflict between the two species eventually brought dragons to thc brink of extinction. For sorcerers who practice witchcraft and the preparation of various elixirs, the dragon carcass is a subject of special interest. His brain, teeth, blood, and various internal organs are widely used by them in laboratories and are welcome goods in the shops of sellers. The tail is used in cooking, where it is highly appreciated by gourmets.

General Information

Appearance: Huge flyable dragons make all living things tremble. Strong claws and paws, a powerful tail, the ability to breathe out fire, steam, spit acid - all this makes the dragon a dangerous enemy.

There are several types of dragons:

- **Green** - The scales are gray, the most common type.

- **Rocky** - Extinct long before the events of the Saga.
- **Black** - The scales are dark brown in color.
- **Red** - The scales are reddish or brick-colored.
- **White** - Dwells in the Far North.
- **Golden** - The scales have a golden hue, the rarest and most legendary dragon-type capable of transforming into anything and anyone (even a human).

9.11 UNICORNS

The Unicorns are a race of sentient beings who came to the world after the Conjunction of the Spheres. They look like horses with a spiral horn on their foreheads. They use telepathy for communication and easily pass through parallel realities and time.

Unicorn horn is a universal antidote. They come in different colors and change color with age. Unicorns do not tolerate the presence of elves, in particular Aen Elle. The Elves, later called Aen Elle, in particular Avallac'h, tricked the unicorns into opening Ard Caeth (the gate between worlds), and then subdued the people living in the new world, killing all the recalcitrant ones. The mythical animal was officially declared extinct in Northern Kingdoms.

10. MAIN CHARACTERS

An important part of the Witcher's universe is colorful characters with a well-developed biography and their own view of events. This section provides information about the key characters in this universe.

* * *

10.1 GERALT OF RIVIA

Geralt of Rivia is the protagonist of The Witcher Saga and subsequent games, a Witcher, a monster hunter, one of the best swordsmen in the North. He has a romantic interest in two sorceresses: Triss and Yennefer. His best friends, in addition to the Witchers from the Wolf School, are the bard Dandelion, the dwarf Zoltan Chivay, and the high vampire Emiel Regis.

Appearance

Geralt is described as a tall, thin, unnaturally pale "not young and not old" man with completely gray, like milk, hair, in books intercepted on his forehead with a leather band, while in games, he has it in a ponytail on the back of his head. He has yellow phosphorescent eyes with vertical pupils. Yennefer describes him as peculiarly handsome, but many other characters in the Saga say that Geralt's face is unpleasant.

Origin

Geralt's mother was the sorceress, or rather, the healer Visenna and his possible father were the mercenary Korin (Andrzej Sapkowski did not recognize this fact as canonical). After birth, the mother gave the boy to the Witchers from the school of the Wolf for education, but before that, she managed to give him a name. During training, Vesemir, a fencing teacher in Kaer Morhen, became the named father and mentor of Geralt.

Approximately 20 years later, when Geralt first entered the "high road" as an adult Witcher, he began to introduce himself as "Geralt of Rivia." The young Witcher received this name on the advice of Vesemir, after he dissuaded him from using the name "Geralt Roger Eric du Ho-Bellegard." Subsequently, the White Wolf even learned to imitate the Rivian accent since potential customers trusted the person from Rivia more than "an oddball from nowhere."

Personal Data

Geralt has a noteworthy, though extremely obnoxious character. The years spent on the highway among various kinds and degrees of marginal personalities, wandering around the world, countless fights and scrapes developed several qualities that allowed him to survive and come out a relative winner from any situation during his adventures. The main character traits of the Witcher are restraint, straightforwardness, honesty, taciturnity, eloquence, curiosity, prudence, secrecy, moderation in everything and the ability not to lose self-control in any situation. By virtue of "innate opportunism" to adapt to any conditions, Gerald is also experienced and practical, unpretentious and independent. In addition, he is distinguished by the strongest humanism, although he does not harbor illusions about the world. Despite the tendency to vagrancy and the inability to live in one place for a long time, which is associated with both character traits and lifestyle, Geralt highly values home and comforts, not giving them up whenever possible. Nevertheless, despite all his foresight and a certain degree of wisdom, Geralt is sharp-tongued, rude, sarcastic, and generally has a specific sense of humor.

According to Dandelion, Geralt is a complete contradiction: despite the relatively high fees for the killed monsters, he always has no money; despite the maintained neutrality, he is always in the thick of events and intrigues; despite the unsightly appearance, ragged clothes, and bad character, he always enjoys a downright supernatural success with the opposite sex; despite all attempts to avoid bloodshed and generally non-conflicting nature, he is a professional and very skillful assassin, who is constantly forced to use his sword for its intended purpose.

10.2 CIRILLA FIONA ELEN RIANNON

Cirilla Fiona Elen Riannon is the heroine of The Witcher Saga by Andrzej Sapkowski. Child of the Elder Blood, a descendant of Lara Dorren.

Origin

Cirilla was born in May 1252 in the family of the fifteen-year-old Princess Pavetta and her husband Duny. To the delight of all, the girl is growing up very lively and active. In addition, she has inherited her mother's beauty, reflected in her refined face, large green eyes typical of their family, and ash-gray hair, all of which promised to make her an enviable bride. Ignoring the usual activities of girls of her position and age, she increasingly prefers the company of boys of her own age, with whom she spends most of her time playing their games.

From a young age, Ciri travels between kingdoms. Many times while still quite small, together with her grandmother, she set off on a voyage to the Skellige Islands to her uncle Crach an Craite, where she stayed for a long time. When she turns about five years old, her parents disappear into the sea, and her grandmother, angry with the jarl of the islands, forbids her to visit the islands she has already loved so much. But Ciri didn't mind too much. The only person left with her is her grandmother, and she gets attached to her, admires her, and tries to be like her in everything. In addition, the disfavor of the lioness from Cintra lasted only six months. Then again, the girl spends many months on the Islands.

From an early age, her nannies tell that she is a child of Surprise destined for a certain white-haired Witcher. The girl sees that her grandmother Kalante does not like this gossip very much, but the more she scolds the nannies for such stories, the more confidence in little Ciri is strengthened that the stories they told are true...

Additionally

- Ciri became the only child who, without being subjected to mutations, nevertheless earned the right to be called a Witcher - thanks to her superpowers (speed of movement, reaction, and others).
- At the age of 15, her height was 1.75 m, and her weight was 50.8 kg.

10.3 YENNEFER OF VENGERBERG

Yennefer of Vengerberg is one of the main characters in Andrzej Sapkowski's The Witcher Saga. Beloved Geralt of Rivia, in fact, the adoptive mother of Cirilla and part-time talented sorceress.

Appearance

Yennefer appears as a woman of extraordinary beauty - violet eyes burning with fire, luxurious black hair, twisted into tight curls falling over her shoulders and a slender figure. To emphasize attractiveness, she does not hesitate to use magic elixirs.

In clothing, Yennefer prefers a combination of black and white. Around her neck, she wears an obsidian star with active diamonds, a powerful magical artifact. She wears a lilac and gooseberry perfume.

Additionally:

- Yennefer is a quarter elf.
- Yennefer never turns out the lights when she goes to bed.
- Possesses excellent memory for faces and figures.

10.4 DANDELION

Dandelion is Geralt's best friend and constant companion, troubadour and womanizer. Author of collections of poetry, Dandelion is the complete opposite and a striking contrast to Geralt - he is almost unable to stand up for himself, chatty and very loving. Nevertheless, he is not inferior to Geralt in knowledge of life, humor and is often wiser than the Witcher. His favorite image is the image of an eternal child, preoccupied only with momentary joys and concerns.

Dandelion is almost always cheerful and almost always in a good mood. Dandelion is kind to everyone and completely sincere. He is completely devoid of any prejudices about representatives of other races (if they, these same representatives, do not try to destroy him personally in any way). He is very devoted to his friends, so much so that in critical situations, he will not feel sorry for himself, he is even prone to stupid and senseless self-sacrifices, at once forgetting about his cowardice.

10.5 TRISS MERIGOLD

Triss Merigold is a sorceress from Maribor, the heroine of The Witcher Saga by writer Andrzej Sapkowski. One of the youngest (she was born about 1235, according to the chronology of the Saga), but at the same time, the most talented sorceress. She is Geralt's lover, as well as the best friend of Yennefer, Ciri and the Witchers from Kaer Morhen.

Appearance

In the book "Blood of the Elves," it is mentioned that she had luxurious brown hair, her pride and "identification mark," a thin waist and penetrating blue eyes. In the choice of clothes, she adhered to dresses without a neckline (this is due to the wounds received on the Battle of Sodden Hill), mainly of blue or green shades.

Game character difference with the literary canon:

- In the game series, the authors forgot that Triss Merigold was seriously injured in the Battle of Sodden Hill - Triss has a scar on her entire chest. If in the literary saga, the sorceress does not allow herself to wear dresses with a neckline after the battle, then in games, there is no wound at all.
- Triss Merigold's hair, according to the literary saga, has a brown hue. In the game series, it has a reddish shade rather than chestnut.
- Triss Merigold has blue eyes, although they are more green in games.

10.6 AVALLAC'H

Avallac'h - elf from people of the Aen Elle. An incredibly powerful magician, who also has the ability to move between worlds using various portals. He occupies a rather high position in the social hierarchy of his People, and is one of the closest friends and associates of the King of Alders - Auberon. In the seventh chapter of the book, "The Tower of the Swallow," an elf signs his rock artwork with an ideogram that looks like a dragonfly.

Appearance

Avallac'h is described as an extremely handsome, tall, and fair-haired elf with a triangular pale face and almond-shaped aquamarine eyes. In the game "The Witcher 3: Wild Hunt," by and large, the peculiarities of the elf's appearance are preserved, except that his hair turns from blond to platinum. He is dressed in navy blue attire of varying lengths, metal bracers, black pants, and brown boots.

The elf does not carry weapons, although, like many magicians in the game, he can materialize a magic staff from the air. Avallac'h also wears a black hood with red lining, to which a light blue brooch is pinned on his chest, a shoulder pad made of turquoise feathers shimmering in blue and green on his right shoulder. For a short time, he wore a metal mask that concealed the "cosmetic" effects of Eredin's curse.

Additionally:

- In chapter 5 of The Lady of the Lake, Eredin Breacc Glas argues that Avallac'h is never wrong.
- Avallac'h, Ge'els, and Auberon all wear the same bracers, but Avallac'h and Ge'els have steel-colored bracers, while the Alder King has golden.

10.7 VERNON ROCHE

Vernon Roche is the leader of the Temerian special unit "Blue Stripes" and the confidant of King Temeria - Foltest. Vernon is a good swordsman. He knows how to shoot a crossbow and does not shy away from using such weapons as daggers. He is a good opponent in fistfights, is quite strong and physically enduring. Possesses outstanding tactical abilities.

Personal Data

This is an example of a person who creates his own destiny. He had tracked Scoia'tael units during the war with Nilfgaard and hung their leaders along the roads. He pulled the elven arrows out of his own body, and soon enough, king Foltest realized that such a man should not be engaged in fighting partisans alone.

Since Temeria has many enemies besides Scoia'tael. Vernon

Roche was noted as an excellent warrior and was promoted to become a special agent. You can say a specialist on special assignments. He carries out assignments that are impossible for others. Roche is a true patriot of his country. He is loyal to Temeria and King Foltest personally since the king saved him from the inglorious life of a drunkard, gave him a job, a title, and the meaning of life.

Vernon does not differ in isolation; he is quite sociable, although he carefully weeds out the circle of his acquaintances. Roche is not restrained, is sharp-tongued and has a specific sense of humor. He is purposeful and believes that in most cases, the end justifies the means. The life truth for Vernon is only one - "either you or you."

As a true patriot of his country, he always tries to work for its good. If he is sent into the fire for the sake of Temeria, he will only ask how long to stay there. Since Vernon became the king's right-hand man, he has uncovered plots, burned the estates of recalcitrant barons, and infiltrated the spy circles of hostile States. Over the years, Vernon has assembled a small team of ruthless thugs, professional interrogators, and silent scouts, who are ready to go to their deaths for him.

Roche is a born leader who skillfully leads his loyal people. His squad has only suffered one setback - he never managed to catch Lorweth, the leader of the Scoia'tael squads.

A lot of stories and fables are told about Vernon. They say that if each of his enemies gives Rosh one oren, he could buy Temeria and even the neighboring lands. And someone says that Roche will have to bury himself in the grave himself because none of his friends will come to the funeral. However, Roche will cope even with this task: it is enough to put a shovel or at least a knife in his coffin.

Origin

Very little is known about Vernon Roche's childhood and youth, but according to his colleague Bianca, we know that Vernon spent his childhood in the deepest poverty, his mother was forced to work as a whore to feed her son, he grew up in a brothel, and he never knew his father. Because of this, the other children disliked him and called him a "bastard." Vernon is still infuriated when this insult is used against him. It is also not clear how or when he joined the Temer army. However, Vernon claimed that King Foltest replaced his father.

Another mystery in the biography of Roche is his meteoric rise up the career ladder and further command of the famous special detachment of the king - "Blue Stripes." It is important to note that Roche was twice awarded the Order of Courage for his valiant service in Temeria. Thanks to his outstanding analytical skills and loyal service to the state, Vernon Roche became a loyal ally of Foltest and one of the most influential people in Vizim and the Kingdom.

10.8 VESEMIR

The oldest and most experienced Witcher on the continent, who is the master of the Wolf School, living in the Northern Kingdoms. The mentor of the legendary Geralt of Rivia. While teaching children at Kaer Morhen, he was a teacher of fencing and monsterology.

Personal Data

For his students, he is a kind of father. He is very warm to each of his pupils, periodically gently teaching life but never refusing to help. Nevertheless, it is not without a sense of humor — subtle and soft, appropriate to the age and ironic perception of less experienced Witchers. And sometimes, he likes to let the fog, pretending to be old and infirm.

He has a surprisingly calm character and is very wise. As a

Witcher, he is very talented and strong — even his considerable years have not slowed down his reaction speed. After the attack on Caer, Morhen became the only elderly Witcher with enough experience to continue teaching the surviving students. However, without knowledge of the secrets of mutagens that turn ordinary boys into Witchers, he is forced to watch as the profession of a professional monster Slayer gradually dies out.

10.9 GAUNTER O'DIMM

Gaunter O'Dimm is a minor character in The Witcher 3: Wild Hunt and the main antagonist of the Hearts of Stone expansion. Also known by the nicknames The Man of Glass and Master Mirror.

Gaunter is a tall man in his forties, with a close-shaven head and short stubble on his face. He has dark brown eyes and dark hair, a Roman nose, and a smiling, round face. Master Mirror is dressed in a yellow short jacket with blue stripes on the shoulders and cuffs, a yellowish shirt, the hem of which protrudes from under the outer clothing, a worn leather hood, leather gloves without fingers, blue trousers with small slits and puffs at the knees, boots.

Personal Data

Gunter O'Dimme is a true trader, flatterer, and excellent negotiator. Possessing an alluring charm, Gaunter can find a way to any heart and charm a person. He appears to be noble, patient, sympathetic, and always ready to help. However, this is just a screen that hides his true face — The Man of Glass is extremely cruel, callous, and vindictive and does not have a drop of sympathy, let alone mercy. And he is ready for anything, just to get what is due under the contracts, or what he wants.

He is willing to make deals with any people, but some (for example, Geralt) are priority purposes for him. Master Mirror always follows the terms of the contract and keeps his word, even if it goes against his own interests (this is a kind of "nobility" of O'Dimme and allows Geralt to win over him). However, this is due to "professional" ethics and practical benefits — people will stop entering into contracts with him if Master Mirror does not fulfill their terms. In addition, it seems that The Man of Glass feels real pleasure from the suffering or torment of people, both physical and spiritual, revels in its power and superiority, and does not value human life at all.

Also worth noting as a personality trait of Gaunter is excitement. It is also his only weakness — twice, people managed to defeat Gaunter, playing on this feature. Pride and narcissism are also the most important qualities of Master Mirror. However, although O'Dimm is flattered by the interest in his person, he is not at all happy with excessive curiosity about himself: "Those who learned my true name are either already dead, or their fate was much, much worse." Despite his entirely negative nature, Master Mirror is not without gratitude and generously rewards Geralt for his help.

Abilities And Skills

The Man of Glass has almost limitless possibilities for changing reality. He is much more powerful than any wizard, and his "spells" do not require any energy or magic formula. Gaunter himself is disdainful of magic, calling it "cheap tricks."

Among the possibilities he demonstrates: control over the passage of time, complete physical and spiritual immortality, weather control, moving through space, telekinesis, creating illusions, creating objects from the air, turning some creatures into others, physically changing objects, including human bodies (leaving scars and marks on the skin, replacing the "living" heart with a stone one), the ability to absorb human souls, mind control, and even an accurate vision of the future.

It is particularly worth noting about the services that Gaunter provides to people in exchange for their souls.

According to his own statement, he is able to give a person everything he wants:

"Grace for body and soul. You will always have plenty of food and drink ... Your body will be as agile as ever. Your passion will charm any woman. Thoughts are faster than lightning. But first of all, I offer you a real adventure. You will experience what only a select few are given to experience."

10.10 ZOLTAN CHIVAY

Zoltan Chivay is a dwarf, businesslike entrepreneur, mercenary, one of Geralt's best friends. The hero of many tavern tales and gossip.

Personal Data

A dwarf, an adventurer, an incorrigible optimist, a convinced altruist, a lover of strong drinks and loud songs, a master of the game of gwent, and above all — a close friend and loyal companion of Jaskier and Geralt — all this is Zoltan Chivay. Their friendship began many years ago when Jaskier and Geralt stumbled upon Zoltan and his company in war-ravaged Riverdell. Since then, their paths have crossed every now and then, and recently, they have become inseparable in both trouble and joy. Zoltan was a partner of Jaskier: they jointly owned the Rosemary and Thyme establishment in Novigrad.

10.11 IMLERITH

Imlerith is an elf of the people of Aen Elle, warlord of the Wild Hunt, and right-hand man of Eredin.

Personal Quality

Imlerith — a powerful and experienced warrior, in battle relied on its huge even by the standards of the elves Aen Elle growth and incredible strength. He was distinguished by an exorbitant vanity, which was expressed in the desire to surpass the enemy in everything and receive honors and privileges appropriate to his position. He wore armor stylized as a human skeleton and was armed with a huge two-handed mace and shield.

Imlerith, the fearsome leader of the Wild Hunt and a frequent hero of The Witcher's nightmares, has long pursued Ciri to deliver her into the hands of his master, Eredin. This powerful and fierce warrior, a participant in countless battles that led Aen Elle in other worlds for many centuries, above all, loved hand-to-hand combat, in which his opponents, fighting for life, could show all their strength, agility, and skill.

10.12 KEIRA METZ

Keira Metz of Carreras — enchantress, blonde, a former adviser to the king of Temeria Foltest. Wears a medallion in the shape of the Egyptian ankh cross.

First appears in the book *Time of Contempt* as a member of a meeting of sorcerers on the island of Thanedd. At a banquet, she meets Geralt of Rivia, who arrived there with Yennefer from Vengerberg. Like other women of her craft, she warned the spook that the other sorceresses were nymphomaniacs and not in their right mind.

During the uprising, she was on the side of the North, participating in catching conspirators. As a result, she broke her leg and rib, as a result of which Geralt took her to a safe place. After that, she was imbued with warm feelings for the Witcher, which Triss immediately noticed.

Personal Data

Geralt met Keira when she literally fell on him from the sky. During the Thanedd riot, Keira was thrown out of a window and nearly fell on the spook's head. The next meeting in the swamps of Velen also surprised him - he did not expect to see a pampered sorceress in the middle of this mud.

Keira Geralt observed what is commonly called the vicissitudes of fate. Once a confidant of the king of Foltest, she was banished from Temeria when she fell out of favor with the king. She later joined the Lodge of Sorceresses, earning the hatred of Emperor Nilfgaard and King Redania. She hid in the Velen wilderness for a long time, posing as a healer, then as an ordinary village witch. It is no exaggeration to say that she hated her position with all her heart.

10.13 LAMBERT

Lambert is the youngest, after Leo, the Witcher Kaer Morhen, one of the representatives of the Wolf School. That is why he is decorated with scars to a much lesser extent than other Witchers. Coached little Ciri, taught her acrobatics and pirouettes.

Personal Data

Lambert, the youngest of the Kaer Morhen Witchers, was known for his audacity and sharp tongue. However, no one could doubt his skill, which he proved by killing monsters from Powiss to Toussaint. He had a reputation for being a bully and a hooligan, and his unusually bad manners even irritated the Witchers who were used to everything.

Nevertheless, everyone knew that Lambert would follow his comrades into fire and water. Although the Witcher did not hide his hatred for Kaer Morhen, when the time came to protect him, he did not hesitate a second.

Additionally:

- Lambert is a skeptic by nature: the author mentions an unpleasant grin that never left his face. He is very cynical and has a short temper. He does not like aristocrats and other rich people.
- Treats magic and all wizards with contempt and distrust. However, despite his obvious distaste for Triss, he found a couple of positive traits in her, which confirms his dislike for magic but not for all its adherents.

10.14 LETHO OF GULET

Letho of Gulet is a Witcher from the school of the Snake, who became famous not only for the extermination of monsters but also for the murder of kings in the name of a good goal. One of the old and loyal friends of Geralt of Rivia.

Appearance

Letho is a muscular, tall, large man with a bald head and short facial stubble. Like all Witchers, Letho has yellow eyes with vertical pupils. He has a huge scar on his forehead in the form of a sharp angle, a short vertical scar that crosses the right eyebrow, and the same one on the right upper lip; he also has a scar on his chin and a small scar on his left cheek.

In addition, his left ear is fractured, and the shoulders and forearms of both hands are covered with burn scars, probably acid.

Letho wears a leather cuirass and a red sleeveless shirt underneath. Around his neck, Kingslayer wears a medallion in the form of an intertwined snake — a sign of belonging to the Witcher school. Letho also has a canvas hood and short fingerless gloves lined with metal pads.

Personal Data

Letho has a very harsh personality; he is tough, cruel, unprincipled but not devoid of a personal code of honor, which, however, is aimed more at personal gain than general altruism.

Kingslayer — an experienced and experienced Witcher who knows the value of himself and his abilities. Letho is reserved in showing emotions, although he does not hide his attitude to certain situations. He is one of the few Witchers who do not complain about their fate. The thug is proud to be a Witcher and enjoys the feeling. He wants to revive the school of the Snake for the sake of his fellow Witchers, who have a very hard time in Nilfgaard.

10.15 MOUSESACK

Mousesack is a druid, advisor, and friend to King Bran in Skellige. The book describes him as a dumpy man with a "whisk" beard. This is a bearded old man, a distinctive feature of which is his ability to predict future events.

Personal Data

Most of the druids of Skellige do Not correspond to the common image on the continent of a white-bearded old man in white clothes, bowing before the Holy oak, taming Wyverns, and pestering the local ruler to include some other animals in the protection lists. Mousesack, an old acquaintance of Geralt, was no exception to the general rule. The tall, thin man was the head of the Druidic circle on Skellig.

In addition, he served as an adviser to the Jarl Crach an Craite in matters of mystical matters and magic, as well as in all other skills other than swinging fists and axes. Mousesack was known for his tenacity and a rare desire for islanders to anticipate all the probable consequences of each act. In general, conversation with him required a lot of time and patience.

10.16 ROACH

Roach is the name of all the horses that the Witcher Geralt of Rivia rides. It should be noted that this is not the same Mare. The horses changed many times during the life of the legendary Witcher, but the nickname was always the same.

10.17 SIGISMUND DIJKSTRA

Sigismund Dijkstra - Former Chief of Redania Intelligence. He calls himself the count, so as not to arouse suspicion and ill-will among the surrounding people, but, in fact, has a low origin, did not even complete his studies at the Oxenfurt Academy and only attended lectures. In the past — the lover of Philippa Eilhart and the lover of the wife of the Minister of Finance Redania Marie de Mercey. Described as an incredibly huge and obese man with a lively mind but not at all like a spy.

Personal Quality

One of the most controversial characters in the book Saga. On the one hand, Dijkstra is a spy, the head of redan intelligence, and certainly a slippery type who is not afraid of intrigue, betrayal, and murder. On the other hand, Dijkstra is perfectly honest — not a single coin has stuck to his hands during his time in power. In addition, Dijkstra is loyal to the one he serves: he was the right hand of the king of Redania Vizimir for a long time and carried out his orders.

After Vizimir's death, Dijkstra and his mistress, the sorceress Philippa Eilhart, effectively ruled Redania. But to his misfortune, he launched an investigation into the king's death, which revealed that he was killed by a group of conspirators, which included Philippa. After learning that her secret was discovered, Philippa sent assassins to Dijkstra, and he had to escape.

Dijkstra and Geralt are quite familiar. During the riot of the sorcerers on Thanedd, Dijkstra pulls the Witcher out of the middle of the mess - of course, not because he loves him very much: he realizes that Geralt is the thread that will lead him to Ciri. Geralt escapes from the spy after breaking his leg. In the third "The Witcher," Dijkstra's leg still hurts. He became one of the shadow rulers of Novigrad.

10.18 EMHYR VAR EMREIS

Emhyr var Emreis is the Emperor of Nilfgaard, the father of Ciri.

Personal Data

Few names in the history of the mainland inspire such high fear and respect as Emhyr var Emreis - White Flame Dancing on Enemy Mounds. Emperor Nilfgaard, lord of Metinna, Ebbing and Gemmera, lord of Nazair and Vicovaro, overlord of half of the known world, hoping to conquer the other half soon. His deeds and thoughts decided the fate of entire kingdoms and peoples.

The emperor ascended the throne in a coup, overthrowing the Usurper in 1257. An excellent warrior and strategist, strong beyond his years, clever, and very cunning. Fluent in Hen Llinge (due to the similarity with the Nilfgaard adverb). He does not unreasonably dislike sorcerers; therefore, he does not even think of giving them at least a fraction of power. He managed to create an excellent army and general staff, an effective government, elevated many capable people, despite their low origin.

Even from the last lost Second war with the nordlings, Emhyr managed to crawl out with dignity: the Empire kept its borders intact and expanded them in some places. Emhyr var Emreis died in the 1290s and was succeeded by Morvran Voorhis.

10.19 ESKEL

Eskel is a Witcher and childhood friend of Geralt. Having passed all the tests of Kaer Morhen with him, Eskel turned into a calm and reasonable Witcher and one of the representatives of the Wolf School. He is not talkative, but he utters every phrase as if verbing global truth. Also like his friend, he considers Vesemir to be his adoptive father. He prefers the western part of the world in his travels. Very strong physically but somewhat inferior in speed to other Witchers. Nevertheless, he puts colossal force into blows.

Personal Data

In many ways, Eskel and Geralt were like brothers. They were the same age, and they had been friends since they had fought with wooden swords in Kaer Morhen. More than once, they received a thrashing from Vesemir for their childish antics. Growing up, each of them chose their own path, but almost every winter they met in Kaer Morhen to spend the winter, drink to their successes, and remember their fallen comrades. And although Eskel was not as famous as Geralt, he was not inferior in experience to White Wolf, and he filled orders for monsters accurately and quickly.

Because of some unpleasant personal memories or for other reasons, Eskel did not like Yennefer and did not trust her but did everything so that this did not affect his friendship with Geralt.

11. BESTIARY

There are a huge number of animals in the world of The Witcher and the question arises — how can people live there at all? This section of the book describes the creatures that inhabit this world.

Witcher's Bestiary is vast and varied. Each creature is dangerous in its own way, but almost everyone is vulnerable to something. Very often, correctly chosen tactics and "methods of influence" help Witchers to pass like a knife through butter in the thick of monsters, while an error can lead to a quick death. Monsters in this bestiary are divided into classes. Fighting each of them is a challenge, and almost everyone needs a special approach. In most cases, the silver blade is most effective against monsters, although there are some more susceptible to steel...

Since there are a huge number of monsters in the Witcher universe, let's look at the most basic ones.

* * *

11.1 THE WITCHERS

The Witchers are sterile mutants with supernatural powers who have been specially trained to become professional monster slayers for hire. It is believed that Witchers have no emotions, although this is not entirely true. Geralt, the central character in the Witcher series, is best known among the Witchers. In recent years, the Witcher caste has dwindled to a handful of active hunters; so few of them remain that the world begins to resemble the times when they were not at all.

The main difference between a Witcher and an ordinary person is his cat-like pupil shape, the Witcher can control the pupil, the eyes glow yellow. This feature gives them the ability to see in the dark and protect their vision from bright light. Witchers have a slow aging process, but they don't live as long as elves and dwarves. They have super-fast reactions, great physical strength and mobility, and have complete control over their breathing and heartbeat.

Witchers are immune to all diseases and most toxins, and because of this, Witchers can take toxic elixirs before a fight that enhance their abilities for a while, while an ordinary person may not be able to bear the effect of the elixir and die. Witchers are characterized by the ability of accelerated regeneration, which gives them the ability to survive after severe wounds that would be fatal to ordinary people.

Witcher Training

Because all Witchers are sterile, they recruit their neophytes from orphans, or, much more often, taking children under the Law of Surprise. At the same time, parents are not always ready to give up their children voluntarily, despite the agreement and the mystical halo surrounding the Witchers.

The preparation of the Witcher takes place in three stages:

The first stage consists of training and a special diet that includes special mushrooms and herbs known only to Witchers, which greatly improve metabolism and accelerate muscle gain.

The second step is Trial of the Grasses (For information about Trial of the Grasses, see the Culture section).

The third stage is the Transmutations. One of the side changes was Geralt's appearance of white (gray) hair. This stage includes the mutation of the eyes. At the same time, the pupils become vertical and the Witchers have the opportunity to see in pitch darkness.

Combat Abilities

Witchers are considered to be among the best swordsman. Their art of wielding a sword in the world created by Andrzej Sapkowski is legendary, and most often with real reasons.

Witcher fencing is a fusion of various schools. If we analyze the fight scenes in the Saga, the real historical schools of fencing are taken as the basis for the school of Witcher fighting.

Although there are enough people and representatives of other races in Sapkowski's world who are masters of various types of weapons, Witchers still occupy their own niche in this area. Their unique combat skills are not only based on years of training but also on the abilities obtained as a result of mutations.

Thanks to their skill, in one-on-one fights or fights with a small group of opponents, Witchers rarely lose. However, there are exceptions to this rule — Geralt, rightfully bearing the status of one of the strongest swordsmen, almost died in the first encounter with the magician Vilgefortz, receiving several serious injuries. In a battle with Geralt, the sorcerer, (possibly with the use of magic) with the help of a staff reinforced with a spell, showed the highest class of fencing. During the fight, Geralt tried four times to strike blows that would have been fatal to any other opponent but not to Vilgefortz - the latter easily parried all four attacks.

In addition to skillful use of melee weapons, Witchers are also known for the skill of hand-to-hand combat. From the descriptions of the scenes of hand-to-hand combat in The Witcher Saga, it can be concluded that Geralt is fluent in the art of unarmed combat, most of all reminiscent of aikido or jiu-jitsu.

Magic Abilities

Unlike combat skills, Witcher magic skills are very limited. For the most part, their magical training is reduced to the theoretical foundations of magic, especially in terms of magical curses and corruption, including methods for removing it. Also, Witchers are very aware of the magical abilities of various monsters.

Witcher Schools

Witchers, perhaps, are an independent caste, almost an order of incredibly strong and hardy fighters. However, several points do not allow Witchers to reach such an honorary title at once. First, Witchers are artificially created. The most complex mutations, training, developing immunity make it possible to survive only a small part of future Witchers. Secondly, their only goal of destruction is monsters that pose a threat to other living creatures. Their representatives can be recognized by the corresponding medallions around their necks.

Notable schools in the world of The Witcher:

- School of the Bear
- School of the Manticore
- School of the Cat
- School of the Viper
- School of the Griffin
- School of the Wolf

There may be other schools, but almost all of them have ceased to exist, but their representatives are scattered around the world.

11.2 MAGIC

Magic is both an art and a manifestation of controlling the forces of primordial Chaos. Magic is available only to sorcerers, priests, druids, witches, but there is a type of magic designed specifically for Witchers — Witcher Signs, for their creation is enough and quite an insignificant gift of magic.

Sometimes, Source-children are born who have truly great power, but their gift is unstable enough that only a few can curb it.

Certain materials block magic, such as Dimeritium.

11.3 WILD HUNT

Wild Hunt is a Horde of phantom riders that suddenly appear in different parts of the world and also suddenly hide. They are considered a symbol of suffering, war, and death.

Rumor has it that they occur mainly, but not only, during the cold period. And the mere presence of the Horsemen causes panic and chaos among the common people, which the Wraiths of Morhogg captures and forces to join their sinister convoy. Numerous stories of missing people and then their unexpected and sudden returns are considered the deeds of the phantom riders. Usually, when abductees return to their native lands, they find only the ancient, overgrown burials of their children.

The narrative of Wild Hunting is not found in the culture of elves and dwarves. This is quite surprising because Older peoples have also dealt with this phenomenon long before the arrival of the human race. But the shorties ignore this phenomenon, and the elves are only mysteriously silent. Among the Witchers, the adepts of the Viper School possess relatively large information about the riders.

Eredin Breacc Glas - the leader of the Wraiths of Morhogg. In the world of humans, the Wild Hunts move on land on horses and using portals, and in the sea, they sail majestically on the legendary ship Naglfar.

Appearance

Wild Hunt is outfitted in the artfully forged and stylized skull and bone armor. Their horses are dressed in blankets embroidered under dragon scales and, like the riders, wear horned helmets on their heads.

These terrifying vestments are specially used by riders, and thanks to them and with the help of magic, they skillfully disguise themselves as ghosts and demons. This creates the effect of intimidation and paralyzes opponents with fear. Often, the hunters did not even have to engage in battle, the opponents themselves ran away.

Additionally:

- Wild Hunt is found in the mythology of the Germanic, British and Scandinavian peoples.
- Against the warriors of the Wild Hunt, as well as against their king, it is more effective to use silver.

11.4 VAMPIRES

Vampires are creatures that appeared on the Continent during a global cataclysm called Conjunction of the Spheres. There are several types of vampires, different in demeanor and habits, as well as abilities and weaknesses.

Animals, especially horses and cats, feel the presence of such creatures. Over the centuries, vampires have been "overgrown" with a vast number of myths that do not correspond to reality, for example, they are not afraid of Holy water, garlic, and aspen stakes.

Vampires fall into several categories: lower vampires, transitional vampires, and superior vampires. Lower vampires are dependent on human blood, susceptible to light and silver, do not have intelligence, obeying instincts. Transitional vampires are sapient but are still addicted to human blood. Higher vampires are intelligent, can feel, have a culture, high intelligence, are not dependent on blood, and generally, are much closer to people than to other vampires.

Lower Vampires

Garkain is a lower vampire, usually found in cemeteries or abandoned buildings. Fleder's "big brother." One of the weakest representatives of his kind but he can easily kill a careless traveler. Like all vampires, Garkain can stun, disorient, or terrify their prey. If successful, he will immediately try to drink the blood of his victim, thereby satisfying his hunger and restoring strength. Against Garkain, the best option for Witchers is to use signs and a silver sword.

Fleder is a lower vampire that most often hunts in urban slums, near cemeteries, or outside human settlements.

Fleder has an extremely ugly head with pointed ears, warty skin, and huge, sharp teeth. It moves hunched over, scratching the ground with its sharp claws on its hind legs. Long, prehensile claws on its feet allow it to hang from the ceiling of a crypt or the wall of a house. Also, a certain danger is represented by the wings of the Fleder, namely paws with sharp claws that allow it to injure its prey.

Fleder is not a very good flyer, the membranes under the paws only allow it to dive at the victim from above. Although he is not especially smart, he knows that such tricks give him an advantage and increase the chances of winning when suddenly attacking unsuspecting victims. Fleders are very sensitive to the sun.

Ekimma is a unique type of lower vampire, which is similar in some habits to Fleder, for example, which leaves terrible lacerations on the victim's body. Perhaps, it lives in hotter or vice versa - in colder areas, unlike most of its other "relatives," who only feel at ease in the temperate climate of the Northern Kingdoms.

Transitional Vampires

Alp is a very rare transitional vampire. Outwardly, the vampire looks like a young girl with large scarlet eyes. The Alps love to feast on the blood of a living victim. They usually attack silently from behind. They can stun their prey with a high-pitched shriek. They are strong, agile, capable of levitation. They settle in city ruins and crypts, easily enduring daylight.

Bruxa is a vampire who has the appearance of a beautiful woman;

however, when she is hungry or attacks, she seems terrible. In the image of a person, it is easy to confuse her with a mermaid, as she has long beautiful hair, sensual eyes, and pale skin.

Bruxs are considered vampires, who are the link between lower and higher vampires. Unlike the lower vampires, Bruxa is intelligent: she can feel, speak, turn into a human, and even love. But unlike the higher ones, Bruxa is still dependent on human blood. An extremely dangerous opponent, she has superhuman strength and can hypnotize her victim. They settle wherever they can survive or subjugate a person to their will. She often looks for a victim who becomes her lover and a source of food at the same time. They are extremely rare, being a relic of the Conjunction of the Spheres.

Katakan is a subtype of a vampire. He has a fairly high level of intelligence. Susceptible to silver. It is not afraid of sunlight, although it is a nocturnal predator. Moves very quickly (both on two and four limbs). They are rarely found, but very dangerous, even for experienced Witchers.

Mula — a humanoid vampire that looks like a little girl, possibly a subspecies of the higher vampire. Appearance is deceptive — this girl can be either ten years old or one hundred and ten years old. A relic of the Conjunction of the Spheres, Mula is a very rare species. During the hunt, she can hypnotize the victim, sing wonderful songs, and whisper soothing words to the victim. She has the ability to transform into a hideous large cat with shabby skin and protruding ribs. Very dangerous opponent.

Higher Vampires

Higher Vampires - vampires of the highest category, one of the most dangerous and powerful creatures found on the Continent. Higher Vampires can be divided into ordinary higher vampires and The Unseens - the most ancient and powerful of them.

11.5 HYBRID

Harpy is a monster with wings like birds of prey and a body that is vaguely similar to that of a woman. She lives mainly in mountainous regions, where she constructs her nests on the slopes of steep rocks. Often attacks victims in a pack.

Griffin is a creature with a body, tail and hind legs like a lion, and head, claws and wings very similar to an eagle. This creature is deadly and extremely hostile to humans. They settle high in the mountains and, like birds, build nests and lay eggs.

Griffin fiercely guards its hunting grounds, often patrolling his territory. They fiercely attack anyone who invades their area of control Griffins — very dangerous opponents, do not underestimate their strength. Stubborn and aggressive, they are deadly with their ability to fly high in the middle of battle and fall like a stone on their enemies, knocking them to the ground and shredding them to shreds with their beak and claws. It feeds on large animals, such as cattle.

Manticore is a giant beast with the body of a lion, large bat wings and a tail similar to that of a scorpion. They are very rare and pose a great threat. It is known that Geralt killed one manticore during the first war with Nilfgaard. The order for manticore was estimated by the Witcher at 150 crowns.

Siren-in many ways similar to the mermaid, the siren is a representative of the ancient forgotten sea people. They use a singsong version of Elder Speech to communicate, but they may also know the general language. They live in water but can briefly go out on land and breathe air.

Succubus-a creature that visits young men at night and causes them to have voluptuous dreams. Unlike other monsters, a succubus is not driven by a desire to kill: they don't want our meat and blood, and often they don't even want to hurt us. They are driven by one thing-boundless lust, which they unsuccessfully try to satisfy, using males of other species, most often-people, and elves for this purpose, who, it should be noted, rarely resist them. This does not mean that succubus does not pose any danger. Their constant pleasantries and caresses, although at first seem pleasant, eventually drove many to madness and even to death.

11.6 MAGICAL CREATURES

Bang and Bue is the result of a magical cross between ogres and trolls. Minions of Sorel Degerlund. Geralt met them in the dungeons of the Ortolan laboratory.

Viy of Maribor-creation of the wizard Alzur. The monster destroyed half of the city of Maribor and escaped into the forest. It is unlikely that the monster gave offspring to survive and preserve the genus. A huge creature with many legs, which makes Viy look like a scolopendromorph, only of gigantic size.

Golem is a huge creature made of stone or clay and animated with magic. Deprived of personal free will, all his actions are aimed at fulfilling the will of his creator. Usually, golems serve as a guard for a mage or some place.

Golem often looks like a clumsy, faceless clay or stone figure. Golem is a piece of rough hewn stone, inspired by the power of magic through its obsidian heart, which is placed by the creator of this creature inside the chest of Golem. The mages who create golems rarely have the talent of a sculptor, they care little about the aesthetic side and focus entirely on functionality.

These creatures must work and protect their master and his property, and golems perform these tasks (especially the last one) just perfectly, with ruthless efficiency. The Golem can only be stopped by its Creator. Most often, the magician sets a golem in motion by means of lightning, so a strong electric shock can also stop or even destroy the golem.

Treant are druid-enchanted oaks that guard the borders of the sanctuary in the forest of Caer Myrkvid on the border of Toussaint and catch intruders.

Koshchey-an artificially created monster not found in nature; it can only appear when it is created by a powerful wizard.

On a flat four-set carcass covered with earthy-rusty and rough hair, there are four pairs of legs, while the fifth head pair of disproportionately long limbs is armed with pincers covered with sharp needles and horn protrusions. It easily tracks prey with its eyes located on the appendages rising from the body and swallows it with its sickle-shaped jaws. The entire body is covered with a strong chitinous carapace.

This is a mythical creature generated by magic, and only the most powerful wizards familiar with the works of Alzur are able to create and manage koshcheys. Externally, it is a mixture of cancer and spider.

Idr is a creature featured in the first chapter of the Season of Storms book. Idr looks like a giant grasshopper. The body color is gray, which provides a good disguise. The Idr body consists of armored segments. The Idr's limbs allow him to move quickly and jump quite far. Planning an attack on the victim is built on an instinctive level, which is well described in the book.

11.7 WRAITHS

Barghest is a wraith who comes to this world from the other world only after he has been called here. It is believed that after unavenged death, the soul returns to this world in the form of a ghostly dog or barghest. According to the plot of one legend, the barghests sprung when one hound breeder was brutally killed. And the barghests didn't disappear until the last of the beater's killers died. The spirit most often takes the form of a black dog surrounded by a ghostly glow, with burning eyes, huge claws, and fangs.

Banshee-a monster whose howl supposedly portends death. She looks like a thin, pale woman with glowing red eyes, dressed in gray rags.

Draug is a monster, an arch-ghost. As an arch-ghost, Draug doesn't have to do anything on his own. For this, he has servants. They are always simple wraiths, cursed souls, and other restless spirits. A king or chief during life, after death, Draug retains his charisma, and his dead subordinates always blindly obey him.

On the way to the underground Palace, a fortress in the desert, or any other gloomy dwelling, the hero must first kill the draug henchmen. Only then can he face off with Draug itself. Such are the legends. The leader of the wraiths is so powerful that he only mocks at simple Witcher tricks. The only sure weapon in the fight against him is the silver sword.

Draugir is a wraith, a warrior of the Draug army. They were brought back to life at the behest of Draug from ancient fields of battle or cemeteries. Draugir obeys Draug's orders unquestioningly. They feel neither fear nor pain. They don't know fear and they can't be put to flight. They are ideal warriors.

Plague Maiden is a monster that is a powerful wraith of a deceased woman.

Noonwraith-this type of wraith occurs on a clear and fine day when the sun is high. Akin to nightwraiths, which only appear at night, Noonwraith looks like a haggard and mournful girl, with very tanned skin and long white hair. Her eyelids are sewn with coarse thread, and she is dressed in a tattered white dress. In the group — a very dangerous and serious opponent, even for a Witcher. Alone - she is not so dangerous.

Swaying ears of wheat in the fields on a windless day inform the arrival of noonwraiths. They lead a round dance in the light of day and try to attract the peasants to their circle. No one ever came out of the circle alive. Noonwraiths mainly inhabit fields and meadows, where they appear around noon. Noonwraith is the kind of wraith who still have a powerful connection to the real world; they can see mortals.

Wraith-the soul of a person or non-human who died a violent death, which cannot find peace after death. Wraith is a sinister creature that the average person doesn't see. This is because this creature is otherworldly and has no real body.

Only Witchers or powerful wizards can see the wraith. Sometimes, Witchers are summoned to exterminate wraiths who haunt the living. Wraiths spawn near cemeteries or in the houses they inhabited during their lifetime. As a rule, they do not remember anything and are distinguished by a very strong hatred of the living.

11.8 RELICTS

Fiend - a huge mountain of muscle and bone, topped with branching horns on the head. Fiends have four limbs that they walk on. They have three open eyes on their foreheads. Depending on the region of their habitat, they have different colors: from dark green to gray or brown.

Crones are a trio of ancient creatures. The Weavess, Brewess, and Whispess reign supreme over the Crookback Bog and control the entire Velen, commanding the people here who worship them as deities. Once a year, they host a fete at Bald Mountain. In the guise of beautiful and sexy girls, every few years, they come to the peasants during the holiday to help them solve any problem.

Godling-in Polish mythology, the ghost of a child who died before baptism. Godlings are forest creatures that live in burrows and rotten tree stumps, always near human settlements. In their behavior and appearance, they very much resemble children, and just like children, they love games and pranks. Godlings are tied to their territory and try to protect everything that lives on it. They help both animals and people, but being timid by nature, they try to help secretly, without attracting attention to themselves. Godlings love such human qualities as joy and naivety, so they love children and often open up to them.

Leshy is a creature that inhabits dense forests. Leshys used to be very common and ubiquitous. Now it is a rarity. Leshys usually feed on forest animals without touching a human. But if a two-legged alien, appearing in the forest, offends nature, the leshy will not wait (especially when hungry) – it creeps up and wrings his neck, or smashes the head with a dry, bony fist. Sometimes, this revered creature can heal other forest dwellers and call them to protect the forest. His attacks are slow but deadly.

Silvan is an extremely rare and intelligent creature that loves to play practical jokes on people. Silvans are very similar to humans, not only in appearance but also in behavior, although it must be said that they have accepted more of our vices and weaknesses than our strengths. Lazy by nature, they would love to spend every day celebrating, smoking pipes, and getting fat on fine foods.

Shaelmaar — a large relict monster that leads an underground lifestyle. It has two-toed forelegs that are used as shovels. The entire body of the shaelmaar is covered with a shell, except for the belly. The monster is blind, but it has excellent hearing. So the best tactic when facing this monster is to place something heavy and noisy against the nearest boulder or a stronger wall, and then silently pray that shaelmaar will roll towards the sound and smash himself against the obstacle.

11.9 CURSED

Archespore — a carnivorous plant, hiding under the surface of the earth during the day and crawling out of hiding and attacking any living creature at night. They say that archespores appear either in places where particularly violent murders are committed or on the graves of victims of such crimes. According to legend, archespores grow wherever terrible crimes occurred, but in practice, they grow mainly in wetlands. Their spores can be spread both by the wind and the unfortunate victims of these predatory plants. Archespore shoots poisonous spikes. In the roots of archespores, you can often see the human body, which may have become the source of rumors and legends about these plants.

Botchling is a cursed creature made from a dead unwanted child who was not even properly buried after death.

Striga is a woman who turned into a monster as a result of a curse. The curse can be removed from the monster, but usually, people hire Witchers to kill monsters and not heal them. Striga is filled with hatred towards all living beings; therefore it destroys them and devours their bodies. The creature needs shelter during the daytime, so it most often chooses abandoned crypts and underground ruins as its lair. Striga is a very strong and agile opponent but not as persistent as it might seem. The monster attacks from ambush and tries to tear the enemies to pieces before they come to their senses and begin to defend themselves. It gets stronger near its lair.

Uma is a character in the Witcher 3: Wild Hunt. An ugly dwarf who fell victim to a curse. Uma appears off the coast of Skellige, where he is found by a local fisherman and loses it to Bloody

Baron cards. Uma amuses the people of Baron with herself and does not cause any trouble. When Geralt learns that this freak is the victim of a curse and is a key figure in the search for Ciri, the Witcher takes Uma with him to Kaer Morhen in order to disenchant.

12. MAP OF THE WORLD

Even though there are no official maps of this universe, fans have created several maps all on their own. According to the author of these series, Andrzej Sapkowski, the current maps are pretty much accurate, and he refers to a version that was made by Stanislav Komárek, who is a Czech translator.

The Continent has four regions. Firstly, the Northern Kingdoms is where the majority of the stories take place. It consists of Cidaris, Aedirn, Hengfors, Cintra, Kerack, Kaedwen, League, Poviss and Kovir, Rivia and Lyria, Redania, Verden and Temeria, including several minor principalities and duchies, like Ellander or Bremervoord. Secondly, the Nilfgaard Empire mostly occupies the southern area of the Northern Kingdoms. Moreover, the Continent's eastern region, like Zerrikania, the Fiery Mountains, Hakland, and the Korath desert, are mostly unknown. This series also mentions some overseas countries that trade with the Northern Kingdoms, such as Hannu, Zangvebar, Barsa, and Ofir.

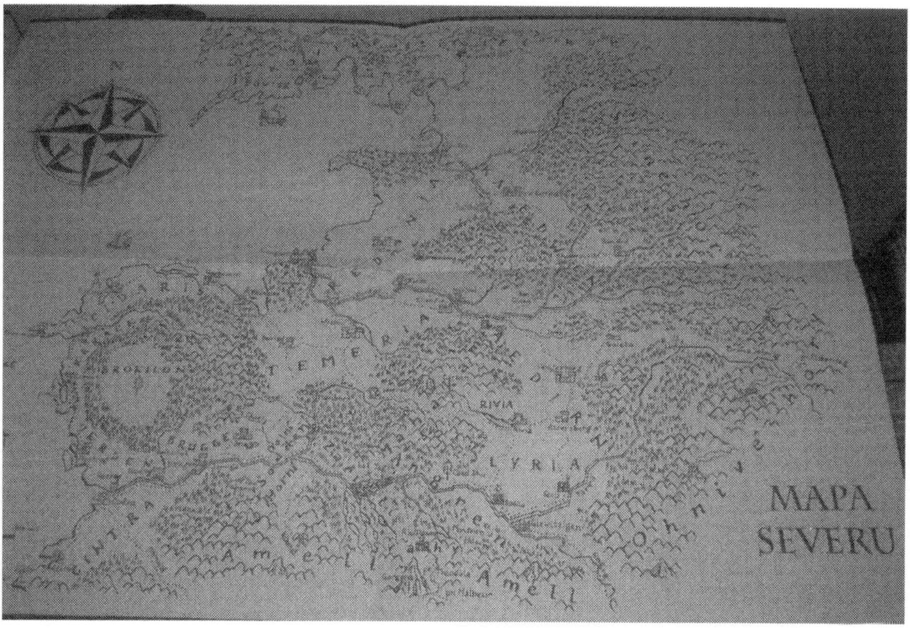
MAPA
SEVERU
TEMERIA
BROKILON
RIVIA
LYRIA

13. GEOGRAPHY

This section describes the main kingdoms, provinces, duchies, and cities.

You can see their location on the map in the Map section. In this section, the main features of geographic objects, their population, and economy will be described. So, in the process of getting acquainted with the work of Sapkowski, you'll have an idea of what location the author writes about, and where visually on the map and among which society the main characters are.

This will make the novels easier to understand and enable you to better understand them.

✻ ✻ ✻

13.1 VERDEN

Just before the war (Northern War II), the then king of Verdun, Ervyll, fearing the aggressive policies of Temeria, recognized the protectorate and made an Alliance with the Nilfgaard Empire. The Kingdom became a vassal of Nilfgaard and, if necessary, was obliged to provide military support to the Empire.

However, soon riots and rebellions began to break out in the country, and, as a result, King Ervyll abdicated in favor of his son Kistrin, who expressed a desire to support the Northern Kingdoms in the war. The alliance with Nilfgaard came to an end. Later on, Verden repelled several attacks by the army of "black." After the Battle of Brenna and the conclusion of an alliance between the Empire and the kingdoms, Verden regained its sovereignty.

Armed Forces

Despite not being the largest territory among the Northern Realms, Verden is a valuable ally and a dangerous enemy. The Kingdom has a strong army.

Economy

Verden, like other coastal countries, builds its economy on fishing, seafood trade, and possibly shipbuilding. Besides, this Kingdom actively mines pearls, amber and rapidly developing agriculture.

Culture

The culture of the coastal state is certainly associated with the sea and marine life.

13.2 THE NILFGAARD EMPIRE

The Nilfgaard Empire is the largest and arguably the most powerful human state in the known world. Having conquered all the lands south of the Yaruga River by fire and sword, the former small kingdom turned into an empire that knows no equal in history in less than a century and a half.

Nilfgaard has a population of about 56 million, and this number is steadily growing despite social and natural disasters. Often, several million people at once become inhabitants of the empire after the annexation of new lands. In 1274 A.D. Nilfgaard occupied more than 50% of the entire known territory of the Continent from the Yaruga River in the north to the borders of the True Nilfgaard (metropolis) in the south, and from the coast of the Great Sea in the west to the Tir Tochair mountain range in the east.

After the last two wars, the empire includes 14 provinces, not counting the metropolis. Each province is essentially a former independent kingdom. After joining the empire, the conquered state receives the status of a principality or a duchy (legally, the statuses are equal), and its ruler becomes an imperial prince. If the line of the imperial prince is interrupted, the Principality is governed by a prefect appointed by the Emperor himself until a successor is elected. Imperial princes report personally to the emperor and have a voice in the imperial senate.

The three provinces enjoy special privileges and retain formal independence from the Empire, as well as their former status, coat of arms, and title of rulers, as a reward for voluntary vassalage from Nilfgaard. These provinces are the Principality of Toussaint, the Kingdom of Ebbing, and the Kingdom of Maecht.

The capital of the empire is the City of Golden Towers. Majestic and mighty, this city is the true center of the world. All the power, all the wealth, and the very spirit of Nilfgaard are concentrated in the capital and are embodied in a hundred gilded spires and domes, over which foreign banners have never been raised. The Imperial Palace, the Patriarchal Temple of the Cult of the Great Sun, the Imperial Military Academy, the Imperial Academy of Magic, as well as the Merchant Guild - all the highest state apparatus is assembled in the City. Equally important is the capital's port, where ships come from all over the world every day and where the strike squadron of the Imperial fleet is anchored. The capital of Nilfgraad is rightfully considered a wonder of the world and the pearl of the Continent.

Additionally:

- The famous lemon vodka is produced at Nilfgaard.
- The history of the Empire depends on the choice of Geralt's side in The Witcher 3: Wild Hunt. In one case, Nilfgaard will absorb the Northern Kingdoms, in another, the Empire will be defeated and lose the conquered lands.

13.3 KOVIR AND POVISS

Kovir and Poviss are one of the Northern Kingdoms. The state has two capitals: winter and summer and is the largest exporter of minerals. Despite not the largest area of possessions, the kingdom is very rich.

Armed Forces

We don't know the exact number of soldiers. It can be assumed that it will not be difficult for the Kingdom to pay for a professional mercenary army. Moreover, in the past, the Kovir monarchs have already resorted to such services of mercenaries.

Economy

Kovir and Poviss is the richest kingdom in the North. The mining of metal ores (mainly precious), salt, glass is developed here. The state conducts large-scale trade with its neighbors, which, of course, brings a lot of money to the royal treasury. Most of the countries in the North are dependent on supplies from Kovir and Poviss. Also, it is worth noting that the quality of the goods is very high, and the art of making weapons is second only to Mahakam. But the main source of wealth is gold; 80% of the world's reserves are located in Kovir. It is no wonder that the state and people are flourishing. For example, the earnings of Kovir artisans are four times higher than those of their fellows in Redania and Temeria. The economy is so developed that even the Nilfgaard empire has to reckon with the distant northern kingdom.

Culture

Kovir has trained many famous poets, statesmen, and military leaders. Here are the bases of the trading guilds of the richest merchants and artisans. Famous sorcerers and sorceresses were also born in this area.

Additionally:

1. Kovir scouts are among the best in the world.
2. A lot of wizards came out of Kovir.
3. Perhaps there was a Witcher school for Cats in Poviss.

13.4 KINGDOM OF SKELLIGE ISLANDS

Kingdom of Skellige Islands is a state located on the archipelago of the same name. These places are shrouded in ancient legends. The inhabitants of Skellige are known as formidable pirates and have a strong fleet, perhaps the best of all the Northern Kingdoms. The archipelago consists of twenty islands, the largest of which is called Ard Skellig. The capital of the kingdom - Kaer Trolde is located on it.

Social Structure

The Skellige Islands have an elective monarchy institution. The head of the state is called the king and rules for life. He is chosen by the council of jarls from among applicants gathered from many clans. Power is often held in one family. Clans, in turn, vary in size and influence. Numerous internal problems often escalate into open hostilities between clans. There is no clear social division on the islands, people are simultaneously peasants, warriors, and sailors, and, therefore, Skellige is perhaps the only state in which the voice of a peasant can be decisive when choosing a jarl.

Armed Forces

Skellige has a strong and numerous fleet, consisting of battle drakkars. Skellige warriors go into battle without a drop of fear and compassion for the enemy. Perhaps the army of the archipelago is not so numerous, but it is definitely not the worst (and maybe better) prepared than the troops of other kingdoms of the North.

Climate

Skellige has a rather cold and damp climate. The weather in the archipelago is rapidly changing and teeming with both rains and gusty winds.

Additionally:

- Skellige is home to the best Gwent players.
- Probably, Scandinavia served as the prototype for Skellige. From there, the way of life (sea raids), division into clans, mythology, names, etc. were taken.

13.5 REDANIA

Redania is one of the largest Northern kingdoms. Redania is home to the Free City of Novigrad and the famous Oxenfurt. Redania is a very rich and powerful Kingdom located in the North. Its strength and power gained gradually. Redania gained the greatest power under King Radovid V (this powerful ruler, who did a lot for his country, was feared even by Nilfgaard). After the recognition of Kovir's independence, the economy of Redania was badly shaken, but it still remains one of the most influential in the North.

After the murder of King Vizimir (Radovid V's father), a hidden dual power was temporarily established in the country, under the screen of the Regency Council, carried out by the head of the intelligence service Sigismund Dijkstra and the sorceress Philippa Eilhart, the head of the Lodge of Sorceresses, and also the mistress of Dijkstra.

After her unsuccessful attempt on the latter and his flight to Zerrikania, Philippa formally ruled the entire Kingdom, almost bringing it to a state of feudal fragmentation. When Radovid matured, he blinded Eilhart, accused her of killing her father, and took the Kingdom under his strict control, then almost all the Northern Kingdoms realized the full power of Redania and began to fear it.

It was on the Redanian regiments, located in the center of the formation in the glorious battle of Brenna, that the main blow of the Nilfgaard fell. The Redanians made repeated attempts to conquer the rebellious county of Kovir (unsuccessfully) and were eventually forced to recognize the independence of Kovir. In 1272, the territories of Redania began to be hunted for witches, sorcerers, alchemists, herbalists, and dopplers, who were burned at the stake.

13.6 TEMERIA

Temeria is one of the most powerful and large Northern Kingdoms, which has great political and strategic significance in the world of the Witcher. The capital is located at Lake Vizima, actually the same name and the capital. Temeria is home to the order of the Flaming Rose. Temeria is home to not only humans but also dryads, gnomes, dwarves, and elves. After the bloody war with Nilfgaard, all sorts of monsters appeared in many territories of the Kingdom, which had never been particularly dangerous before. And many routes have become unsafe due to the huge number of bandits and robbers. Under the protectorate of Temeria is a lot of lands, the number of vassal States Temerians occupy second place in the world after Nilfgaard.

Military Establishment

At the Battle of Brenna, the Temerian forces, supported by Redania, were the center of a united Nordling army of about 18,000 soldiers. Thus, we can conclude that Temeria itself fielded about 11,000 soldiers. At the beginning of the war, the Temerian army numbered about 27,000 poorly trained recruits, of little use for battle (Battle of Maribor), and at the end, about 50,000 veterans, thanks to whom Temeria was able to expand its borders. Currently, the number of Temerian troops is unknown, but it is probably the most numerous army in the North.

Special Forces

Temeria has a special unit "Blue Stripes," created specifically for the fight against "squirrels." The number of the squad is unknown, although it is known that there are not so many people in the "Blue Stripes," The main commander of the special unit is Vernon Roche, a close friend of King Foltest.

Economy

Temeria is quite a rich Kingdom but not like Kovir. The basis of the economy is the production and cultivation of various products and goods. Trade and mining of valuable minerals, ores, and precious metals, which are extracted from the Mahakam mountains, is also developed. But with all this, because of the war, there was a drop in the rate of the Temerian Oren.

Culture

The population of Temeria is mostly politc, educated, religiously and God-fearing, but does not recognize the representatives of the Elder Nations. Most Temeria residents are racist. This country is also home to many powerful sorcerers and famous travelers.

13.7 OXENFURT ACADEMY

Oxenfurt Academy is a renowned institution of higher education located in Redania, in the city of Oxenfurt. It is one of the best universities in the Continent (like the Imperial Academy in Nilfgaard) and is a coveted educational institution for people from all over the world, even from across the Great Sea - from Ofir and Zangwebar.

In the book "Blood of the Elves," the academy first appears before the readers. She also appears as a location in front of players in the Hearts of Stone expansion.

The Academy has restored the elven aqueduct, which now acts as an experimental plant for wastewater treatment and filtration.

The library of the Academy is a place of pilgrimage for scientists and researchers from all over the world. The library of the academy contains ancient scrolls from the time of the Conjunction of the Spheres, old elven manuscripts, dwarven encyclopedias, treasure maps, scientific works, and graduation works of all students who have ever studied at this institution.

13.8 KAER MORHEN

Kaer Morhen is a citadel that housed a school for training Witchers for many centuries. The name of the fortress comes from the Elder Speech, where Caer a'Muirehen is translated as "Fortress of the Old Sea." She is the so-called Wolf School, one of the six famous witch schools.

The path to the fortress lies between the high cliffs of the mountain range. Having found a barely noticeable gap, the traveler enters a tunnel, which expands over time, and upon leaving, his gaze opens the view of a rocky valley surrounded by mountains and a fortress hidden in it. In the forest, located near the citadel, there is a winding, barely noticeable path, called by young Witchers nothing else but "The Killer" for all its complexity and danger. On the trail, the young students improved their running speed and developed breathing control.

14. FEATURES OF THE FICTION

The "Witcher" series refers to the subgenre of "postmodern" fantasy — a direction that is very different in general stylistics from the fantasy "canons" given by works in the "epic" fantasy subgenre and representing a more rigid and naturalistic variety.

The author retains the traditional for fantasy scenery in the style of the Late Middle Ages. However, the way of thinking of the characters, their psychology, experiences, and motivations often deliberately contradict the environment in which they are placed by the author's idea and rather correspond to our contemporaries. The same goes for the issues raised in the work that is quite relevant to the modern reader: the progress and price paid for it, the pressure of civilization on the environment, the clash of civilizations, race intolerance, genocide.

The structure of the fiction's world resembles America after the first wave of European colonization. A strip of land stretching along the western coast of the continent is already sufficiently populated and equipped, the local indigenous population ("savages") — forced to assimilate, driven into reservations and ghettos, or pushed into mountains and other uninhabitable places. However, there are still many "white spots" on the map, even information that reaches Westerners about the human cultures of the East is extremely fragmentary.

There are many fractions in this world - peoples, races, states, organizations and secret societies, fighting for their often self-serving interests, and relations between them and the main characters of the saga are unstable - former allies are easy to turn into enemies, and vice versa. The main characters are constantly caught between two fires, being forced to make a choice in situations where the right path and the right choice simply does not exist.

The author does not divide everything into "black" and "white" but rather paints a picture of his world in various shades of gray, while often resorting to a naturalistic description of the "dark" sides of life, cruelty, violence, and xenophobia. In the final books of the series, anti-war rhetoric is clearly visible, which does not boil down to pacifism and non-resistance to evil.

Non-human races represented in the world of the work — elves, gnomes, halflings (why — see "Bestiary" by Sapkowski) — outwardly, they correspond to the traditional canons of fantasy, but their images are supplemented by many elements that are not typical for the genre. In traditional fantasy, elves are wise and benevolent centenarians. Sapkowski describes them as ancient, almost losing the ability to reproduce, and because of this, they are an endangered race of narcissistic and arrogant creatures. Elves are not inferior to humans in their cruelty and hatred of foreigners; their actions are rather more distinguished by sophisticated cunning than wisdom. Elves partisan groups called "squirrels" terrify the peasants, who are torn between fear of the elves and fear of punishment for helping them.

There is a pronounced romantic line in the work. An important feature - a keen sense of humor, sometimes turning into a satire on the burning issues of our time. The author uses traditional mythological and fairy-tale stories but significantly changes them by weaving into the narrative outline.

15. FROM AN INTERVIEW WITH SAPKOWSKI

"When I became interested in fantastic fiction, I absolutely did not believe in success. Absolutely. There was just some need to write. I wrote in different magazines, even in fishing, and when "Fantastic" magazine announced a contest for the best story, I said to myself, why not? I'll write a story. Why fantasy? I thought that the Poles do not know how to write fantasy, and no one will choose it except me. Okay, I'll write a fantasy. But which one? Tolkien's? I can't — the volume is too limited. Military science fiction like Conan? It's not good. What's left? I had no choice but to remake a fairy tale or legend. And there was a Polish fairy tale about a young shoemaker who came to a certain city, freed it from a monster that killed people, and took the king's daughter as his wife. I said to myself, this is so stupid! These things are not done by shoemakers. Shoemakers sew boots, and such things are done by professionals. And I came up with a professional."

"...I thought that Polish fantasy should have at least one saga. I know I won't write them again. The short form is very complex. You need to fit absolutely everything into eighty pages. It's much easier to write a saga."

"I wanted to write a Polish version of "The Chronicles of Amber." But then I decided - why do we need a second Zelazny? I wanted to write a Polish fantasy. In Poland, no one wrote fantasy before me; there was no tradition. BUT in the series about Geralt, neither Polish nor Slavic mythology is suitable for fantasy. I used something from Tolkien, mostly from the Celtic peoples. But, of course, a little rethought."

"I am a science fiction author, but I live in the real world and write about real issues that disturb people. You can avoid political hints, but people will find them anyway. So I'd rather introduce them consciously."

16. WITCHER LEGENDS

In 2013, the book "The Witcher Legends" was published in Poland - a collection of 8 short stories about the "Witcher world" of Russian and Ukrainian science fiction writers, among them, Andrei Belyanin, Mikhail Uspensky, Maria Galina and others. They were conceived by Wojtek Sedenko and Pawel Laudanski with the knowledge and approval, according to the publisher, of Sapkowski himself — although the writer had not previously given permission for such books.

The collection includes stories about the famous Witcher Geralt, his friend - bard Dandelion, Witcher's beloved - sorceress Yennefer, but along with them, the book includes stories that unfold a few hundred years after the end of the saga, and some are connected with our reality. The anthology is positioned as a fantasy book, a tribute to Andrzej Sapkowski.

17. ADAPTATIONS

From 1993 to 1995, 6 comic books were released, based on Sapkowski's works (written by Maciej Parowski and illustrated by Boguslaw Polch):

1. "The Road with No Return" (Polish: Droga bez powrotu).
2. "Geralt" (Polish: Geralt).
3. "The Lesser Evil" (Polish: Mniejsze zło).
4. "The Last Wish" (Polish: Ostatnie życzenie).
5. "The Bounds of Reason" (Polish: Granica możliwości).
6. "Betrayal" (Polish: Zdrada).

In 2011, the comic book "The Good of the People" came out. The "House of Glass" comic book came out in 2014.

In 2015, "Matters of Conscience" was released — a comic book about the fate of Saskia, Yarpen after the events of the game, "The Witcher 2: Assassins of Kings."

In 2015, the "Fox Children" comic book came out, which is based on the 14th and 15th chapters of the latest novel, "Season of Storms," the content of which has been reinterpreted and thus became independent of the book's plot. The comic book, "Curse of Crows" came out in 2017.

In 2018-2019, the comic book "Of Flesh and Flame" was released.

In 2001, the Polish publishing house, MAG, released a role-playing board game, "The Witcher: The Game of Imagination" (Polish: Wiedźmin: Gra Wyobraźni:) based on "The Witcher" series.

In 2009, the symphonic rock band "ESSE" staged the rock opera "The Road with No Return" and made a film musical of the same name based on the Witcher Saga.

17.1 Computer games

In 1997, Polish video game developer, Adrian Chmielarz, and his then studio, Metropolis, decided to create a computer game on the unfinished "The Witcher" series.

Chmielarz was a fan of the books, was on good terms with Sapkowski, and got his permission to develop the game — the correspondence was in the form of paper letters, as Sapkowski did not use email. For the license for "The Witcher," Chmielarz paid a certain amount, "reasonable for Poland in 1997." After receiving the money, Sapkowski did not respond to new letters from the developer for a long time and then wrote that he didn't care about the game. Chmielarz intended to make a "3D action-adventure" with moral choices, a serious adult storyline, and elaborated characters. Although Metropolis made an early version of the game, such an ambitious project was beyond the reach of a small studio. The early alpha version suffered from many technical problems, and the German publisher, TopWare Interactive, with which the Studio negotiated, was concerned that Sapkowski's books were not so familiar to Western players as to convince them to buy the new product. Ultimately, the project was abandoned and never released.

In 2002, another Polish company, CD Projekt, became interested in "The Witcher." Earlier, the company had opened its own CD Studio, Projekt RED, in Lodz and was looking for a suitable project. Sapkowski again agreed to sell the rights to "The Witcher," asking CD Projekt to settle a possible legal dispute with Metropolis. Although the company offered him a percentage of the sales of the future game, the writer insisted that he was paid the full amount at once. He did not believe in the success of the game and thought that if he agreed to a percentage of the sales, he would not see any money. He later recalled that CD Projekt had brought a "big bag of money" and that was exactly what he expected from the adaptation: "a big bag of money." Adrian Chmielarz and the representative of CD Projekt RED, Sebastian Zielinski, later reported that the sums were not so large — Sapkowski received 15,000 zlotys from Metropolis in 1997 and 35,000 from CD Projekt in 2002.

In the following years, CD Projekt RED has consistently released three computer role-playing games:

- "The Witcher" (2007),
- "The Witcher 2: Assassins of Kings" (2011),
- "The Witcher 3: Wild Hunt" (2015).

Each of these games has consistently gained increasing critical and commercial success. In 2018, a collectible card game, "Gwint: the Witcher" and its offshoot "Blood feud: the Witcher Stories" in the genre of role-playing and card games were released.

17.2 TV series

In 2001 and 2002, a feature-length film and TV series, "The Witcher," directed by Marek Brodský and based on a script by Michał Szczerbic, were released. The role of Geralt was performed by Michał Żebrowski. In fact, the film was a short version of the TV series. Both the film and the series received negative reviews from both critics and fans of Sapkowski's books.

In 2017, Netflix streaming service began developing a TV series based on books about "The Witcher." Eight episodes of the first season of "The Witcher" lasting one hour each were filmed from October 18, 2018, to the end of May 2019. The shooting took place partially in Budapest. Andrzej Sapkowski refused to oversee the project. The role of Geralt was played by British actor Henry Cavill, best known for playing Superman in the DC Extended universe. The first season of "The Witcher" on Netflix was released on December 20, 2019, and got mixed reviews from critics (55% on Rotten Tomatoes), had good ratings, and was renewed for a second season before its release. Andrzej Sapkowski was delighted with the series, especially the game of Henry Cavill. According to the writer, Cavill should forever remain the face of Geralt in the memory of the people.

18. PRAISE FOR THE WITCHER

Sapkowski has a phenomenal gift for narrative, inventing sensational events, creating a suggestive mood, and building up the suspense along with a dazzling, slightly cynical sense of humor (Jacek Sieradzki).

Sapkowski is a genuine stylist (Nerds of a Feather).

Sapkowski is very good at creating interesting, imaginative characters with unusual levels of depth to them ... The Last Wish is an enjoyable book full of stories both melancholy and comic (The Wertzone).

The universe of Sapkowski's The Witcher is one of the most detailed and best-explored in modern fantasy, offering endless opportunities for fresh ideas (B&N).

This beautifully written character-based story from Polish author Andrzej Sapkowski ... a refreshing champion (The Specusphere).

Dear Buyers!

Thank You for purchasing & reading! Hope this can help y'all to love the Witcher as much as I do! Enjoy!

If you leave without writing a review about the guide, one sad author will become more... :)

Ted West.

Printed in Dunstable, United Kingdom

68704013R00085